COMING FOR TO CARRY
(a novel in five parts)

LORRIS ELLIOTT

Published in 1982 by
Williams Wallace
229 College Street
Toronto, Canada
M5T 1R4

Canadian Cataloguing in Publication Data

Elliott, Lorris

Coming for to Carry

ISBN 0-88795-019-1

1. Title

PS8559.L64C65   C813'.54   C82-095209-5

PR9199.3.E44C65

Published with the generous assistance of the Canada Council and the Ontario Arts Council.

Printed and Bound in Canada.

Acknowledgement

"Return to D'Ennery" by Derek Walcott. From, *In A Green Night*, Jonathan Cape Ltd.

The Whole Armour by Wilson Harris, Faber and Faber.

"The Dolt" by Donald Barthelme. From *Unspeakable Practices, Unnatural Acts*, Bantam Books.

"My Girl and the City" by Samuel Selvon. *West Indian Stories*, edited by Andrew Salkery, Faber and Faber.

To my father and mother and all other families and friends without whom this would not have been possible.

Arrived at its anchor of suffering, a grave
Or a bed, despairing in action, we ask
O God, where is our home? For no one will save
The world from itself, though he walk among men,
on such shores. . .

Derek Walcott

Thinking of anything was beyond him. I sympathize.
I myself have these problems. Endings are elusive,
middles are nowhere to be found, but worst of all
is to begin, to begin, to begin.

Donald Barthelme

PART ONE
A Non-beginning

First, let me tell you who I am. Rather, let me introduce myself. My name is Omoh—that is, as far as they have told me. So now the introduction is complete, let me go on to tell my story.

Ah yes, I do remember well, indeed I do. In fact, I remember it all so well that I long to tell it to you—to pour it all out cleanly from my breast. Why? you ask me. You would not believe this, but it is the truth. As if I were some ancient mariner, I feel an itch upon my chin, where stubs of hair protrude. What's more, my eyes are glittering bright. And so, I seek someone to listen to my tale.

I wait, but no one comes. And even if one were to come, I am not sure that he or she would care to listen. I, moreover, would not dare to hinder anyone. But yet, alas! I wait and wait, but no one comes. No bridegroom nor any next of kin. But then, perhaps a bride! A virgin bride to soothe and calm the restless coursing of my fond desire, that I may mount and ride far far into the darkest past—there to discover truths and answers as yet unrealized, and thence to rush straight on into the secret archives of the future to learn what lies ahead for me. Then perhaps, if all bodes well, I may begin to tell my story and, in the telling, learn the why and how.

But no one comes. And though I feel the urge to tell it all, I do not know where to begin and how. And so, I keep on waiting while the seconds tick and tock their merry minuet of time relentlessly. Where to begin and how? That is the question that must be answered now. Indeed, I do not know. That is the God's truth, man, no bullshit.

O.K. O.K., I'm calm again. Let's see. Where to begin and how?

1

"The end is the beginning," I once read. But then, alas! what is the end? Good Lord, I wish that I could give it up. My chin's afire, my aching eyes see nothing as they strain to scan beyond their ordinary ken, my aching limbs scream out and my fragile skull throbs dangerously.

If I could only find a word—the necessary WORD, perhaps it would, by virtue of its very nature, create new words and so evolve my still unstructured tale. But then, I'm sure that such a WORD does not exist today. And even if it does, as in once-upon-a-time days, it must have lost its magic. Perhaps so many hands have touched it into life that it has multiplied itself into pale sterile imitations of itself. And so, I am and will continue to be denied the fruition that I long for.

Enough of this, or else I shall go mad. Christ! I feel my eyes grow dull and heavy with the nothingness that lies before them. My blood no longer stirs the hectic pulse of keen anticipation. Instead, a steady pounding now assaults my ears. Is this—is this indeed my dream horse coming for to carry me? Or, good Lord! some sinister creature of the night? I seem to hear an angry snorting growing louder with each second, and feel the humid air becoming restless as with the rapid swishing of a tail. I seem to see the fiery points of mane glowing strangely from a shimmering neck and smell the acrid sweat and taste the atmosphere now sickly sweet.

Enough! I cannot stand it any longer. Yet I am not afraid. I'll sit right here and wait. But now—how strange! I feel myself being wafted upwards upon a magic carpet of light-headedness and swept away off into dark swirling masses of uncertainty. And now, suspended for a while, I feel myself being to fall, like some ancient youth, plumb down into an ocean of frustration unvisited by tides—an ocean dark but boasting no Homeric vintage. And now—

Good God, I cannot understand, I know nothing more. Go ahead, bust your damned guts. See if I care. Laugh! I cannot tell you where or what or who this self may be. Shit! I know nothing, alas! and so I can no longer tell you anything. So there. Ha ha... ha ha... ha ha. Good God!

PART TWO
An Intervention

I move around in a world of words. Everything that happens is words. But pure expression is nothing. One must build on the things that happen: it is insufficient to say I sat in the Underground and the train hurtled through the darkness . . . . So what? So now I weave . . . .

Samuel Selvon

3

DREAM BEGINS

Ah yes, Omoh remembers it well—perhaps, he remembers it too well, indeed—too well to tell it, that is. And so, he sits there now with elbows folded tight against his chest as if to warm himself, not even hearing the loud humming nor the sometimes knocking of the old typewriter there before him, nor noticing the many books piled high on shelves about him. But he just sits there silently remembering, remembering all and all too well remembering, remembering:

large frosty fluffs of cottonwool falling with frequent 'flooshes' upon roofs already blanketed with snow and a soft but steady sound of 'flooshes' barely perceptible yet like a lullaby like a drug that doesn't stupefy bringing deep sleep deep peaceful sleep indeed

yet life supposed to be now temporarily benumbed by winter's cold bursts forth in all exuberance with children puffed up in soft woollen clothing (colorful as seen in catalogues) prancing sportively about and noticing no one but some hurling round wads of frozen lint and others streaking in loud crazy zigzags down miniature mountain-slides while one busy lad (being Father of the man) intently moulds his Firstborn a large round frosty form with neither arms nor legs yet sweetly smiling

suddenly from out the mountains (Rockies he had been taught to call them) mountains of dread aspect such as once caused some budding poet to blush with guilt for stealing other people's boat and rowing out to sea from out these mountains with their snow-capped tops glistening in the wintery sun there comes a figure dressed in red (he always gets his man and woman too so beautiful he rides in Nelson Eddie style) riding with boyscout hat and lanyard up tall upon a horse

into the children's busy world of fun he rides but they do not cease their actions for he belongs to them so too the mountains and the large rivers (Fraser and Mackenzie he had learnt to call them) rivers in which the salmons fight the rapid downward flow upwards to life and death

the black bears the white ones and the brown ones too standing twelve feet tall and staring blankly at the man in red mushing busily along to find his man and get his woman too

the wide expanse of land far far beyond the mountains with the distant houses and the people glowing with a golden haze upon a golden sea of grain (wheat as the books had named it) a sea that billows gently as the warmer winds blow by

and too—

"Omoh! you fool!"   *DREAM ENDS*

Ah yes, Omoh sits there remembering and hearing once again the piercing cry that shatters for the second time the dream world of his

4

past and present too. The 'flooshes' cease, the fluffs of cotton wool all melt, the happy-smiling child-created form now weeps itself into a pool, as he sits and hears and sees and feels again, remembering all the while.

"Omoh! you fool! the plane leaves in a few hours, and now you can't get up. That's what 'appens when you stay up all night long drinking with dem good-fuh-nuttin' boys." — Mother

"O.K., O.K.," he hears himself reply.

"Thanks be to God you goin' far'way from all dis."

"O.K., I'm getting up," he answers, thinking all the while, now to get up and hurry and get dressed and for the last time perhaps enjoy a cup of hot thick oily cocoa-tea cooled down with fresh cow's milk swimming on the surface and for the last time too perhaps an oily saltfish cake tucked cosily away inside a crusty crackling hopsbread and do all this before the boys come ready for the airport with a good supply of Vat which I hear you can't get up in the big land because it's too hot for the natives there and so to hurry and get dressed and eat something because a man can't drink rum on an empty stomach you know and nothing lines the stomach better than something salt washed down with cocoa-tea and cow's milk straight from the nipples and—

"Omoh!" once again the voice. "You damn deaf or what?" By this time, Ma Poppo has almost fainted with excitement. She's fidgeting like mad. "T'anks to God you getting dis boy 'way from dis drinkin' in dis place," she thinks almost aloud. "Omoh!" once more with vengeance. "Buh wha' wrong wid you, boy?"

This time, however, Ma Poppo struggles bravely to disguise the anxiety she feels as she wonders with a whisper, "Buh wha' as goin' do when he done gone and lef' me? Ah ain't got nobody else to look after me and keep me company. Deep down inside he's got a good heart, he really is a good boy." Mother will miss him.

Her eyes grow moist as she gazes out through the narrow window. Finding no consolation there, she forgets to cry and comes alive once more.

"Dem rascals! You can't trus' dem at all. Dey promise to pick you up and dey should' a been here long time ago. Migod Omoh, you goin' miss the plane."

But Ma Poppo's fears are soon allayed, for the fellows come in time—quite early, island time. The plane leaves in an hour, and the trip to the airport takes at least forty minutes.

They come in two cars and the Vat is flowing freely, despite the early hour. Mildred is in one car and Janice in the other. They are busy 'cutting' eyes at one another. Just then Bignose Melda, small town

5

philosopher, appears, watching with interest from her doorway. Now coming down the steps, she moves closer and peeks into one car and then the other.

"My Gawd!" she finally exclaims, bursting with malice, "Buh look how dese wimen's pouting up! Awl you 'oping to become doctorwife, eh? Well, tek it from me, neider o' yuh goin' be fit to wash 'e socks w'en 'e come back 'ere wid 'e w'ite wife 'anging pon 'is arm. 'eh 'eh 'eh."

Stung with chagrin, Janice blushes as only Blacks can blush. Mildred's eyes blink rapid-firing at Melda who, with her hands on her stomach to hold the six-month foetus firm within her womb, rocks backwards and forwards to the rhythm of her laughter. Fortunately, Omoh appears in time to prevent any further developments. With Ma Poppo leaning on one arm, he slowly makes his way down the steep rickety steps. The tension falls apart, snapped into two. Omoh helps her into one car, then hurries into the other. The doors are quickly shut and, with several jerks and sputters, the mad dash to the airport begins.

As they turn the corner, the sound of Melda's wicked laughter comes after them but suddenly it stops, as a sharp pain strikes home where her hands are poised. Grimacing with ugly consequences, she turns around and slowly makes her way up into her one-room cardboard shack, there to resume her daily task of caring for her five curly-headed piccaninnies.

* * *

All these things Omoh not only remembers well, as he sits before his typewriter, but also sees and hears and feels and thinks again. Indeed, if he could only tell them to you, the incidents would be more accurately rendered—the images much more appropriate, the feelings more profound, the spoken words much more authentic. But he just waits and waits, not knowing how to begin or, having begun, how to continue and to end. Yet, as he has done so many times before, he lives again the joshing and the drinking, the many near mishaps, the intermittent fears he struggled to repress during the frenzied drive to the airport, and too the safe arrival in the midst of boisterous shouts and loud hand-clapping of those there to see him off.

Entering the jam-packed departure room, he feels the Vat begin to hit the spot within his well-lined stomach. Soon a loudspeaker, crackling nervously at first, finds its voice and booms its preliminary summons to the would-be travellers. Assuming an air of nonchalance, Omoh turns to say a last goodbye to his many friends and well-wishers.

A sudden silence hushes up the room. The boys, holding half-empty bottles, stand staring blankly at him as the reality of the situation dawns on them. Mildred and Janice, a sense of common suffering having drawn them closer to each other, are both watery-eyed.

Unable to decide which of his fair ebon ladies he should kiss first and wishing to offend no one, Omoh extends both hands, one to each of them. He struggles desperately to appear the master of the moment, but then he spots Ma Poppo, her head-kerchief removed and held in readiness to mop up the flood of tears she now barely holds back. Knowing well the all-too-well-rehearsed scene that threatens to unfold, he begins to panic. But right then (how unfortunate!) with a crackle and a sputter, another boom summons them to board the plane immediately.

Jolted into action, Omoh brushes a quick kiss across Ma Poppo's cheek, frees his hands from the warm caresses of his two beloveds and pats them each upon the head. Then, turning suddenly, he rushes to the nearest exit, waving frantically to the boys still staring blankly at him. And just before he disappears beyond the gates, he shouts in strange falsetto,

"See ya later fellas."

Now caught within a crush of hot and sweaty bodies that jostle onwards to the ramp, he wishes to look back but doesn't dare. Right at the bottom of the ramp he pauses slightly, thinking, "Oh man, a Viscount! What pleasant colours! And how beautifully they show up against the dark green background of the distant hills, the Three Sisters, a once welcome sight to ancient mariners from far away, but now a—"

A not-so-gentle bump reminds him of his purpose and sends him hustling to the steps. Smiling at the hostess who checks his name, he notes the well-formed curves and gives her full marks without hesitation. Then just as he stumbles awkwardly into the cosy-looking dark red chambers, he hears a distant but familiar sound—the mournful wailing of a saxaphone, an almost painful cry:

> The Trinidad Carniva-a-a-al
> Is the biggest Bacchana-a-al

Boy Mack, Omoh realizes, has shaken off a bitch of a hangover just in time to make it to the airport before the plane takes off.

* * *

Omoh still sits there, eyes staring wide open, not seeing anything that's ahead but remembering, just barely realizing, that the plane is moving and seeing through the window panes the blurred forms of people waving frantically, and feeling a bucking and a rearing as the plane begins to lift its massive bulk up off the tarmac into the air, seeking the distant land. As it strains upwards to the required height, Omoh's eyes begin to shut, for he feels tired now. In fact, he is very tired and longs for sleep, deep peaceful sleep, deep deep peaceful sleep, deep deep— But no sleep comes! Instead, that sound again! the painful wailing of a saxophone! It buzzes strangely in his head, vibrating rapidly and growing in intensity, as his entire self begins to tingle and—

And now he hears the roar of surf that rushes up the sparkling sands and sees it disappear all sucked up by the thirsty shore and feels and tastes the salt sea breezes that come to cool the sun-burnt land, and there is a fragrance too—refreshing! It dries the tears that lurk about the eyes and soothes the burning forehead.

Sweetly smiling now, Omoh lets himself sink deeper and deeper into his reclining seat, alone in his sweet chariot as he zooms skyward on to his paradise and thinking, hardly conscious now, swing low sweet chariot coming for to carry. . . .

But a sudden something thrusts him bolt upright, his eyes full open now. That sound again, vibrating buzzing tingling! And there's more— much more: the sound of ringing steel sweet harmonies tapped out on well-tuned old oil drums by sticks with rubber tips, the rhythmic shuffling of numerous soft-shoe feet, kaleidoscope of colours, cycles of history, fictitious heroes come alive, Caesar and his throng quite undisturbed by thoughts of dull conspiracy and Cleopatra more dusky in an alien sun more hot, Arabs trailing free- flowing multi-coloured robes, Alexander and his hordes. wisemen of the Orient and geisha girls, Indians displaying plumage more brilliant than peacock's, warriors of ancient Africa bristling in mock savagery of tribal warfare, sailors fancy-dressed and delicately balancing large head-pieces of fruits and flowers spiders and lobsters, prehistoric animals, bats and bullfighters, lords ladies employers employees lovers scoundrels, rival gangs, Commandoes bearing strangely silent weapons—the whole mad riot of a two-day reign until King Carnival so rudely wakened on a Monday morning abdicates his throne in honour of a greater King and the foreheads of his many subjects are touched with ashes early on a Wednesday.

"Where am I going? To what strange land? To what cold country?" Omoh shudders, thinking further, "To starve, to get sick, to worsen and to die?" Then smiling, "Silly! how silly to forget the campus and the labs, the lectures on medicine and surgery! And then, of course, to be a doctor, to return home and so to be admired and be loved and envied—yes, envied and perhaps hated too!" Warm with pride, he sees himself breathing new life into some fair creature already given up for dead and whispering, "No thank you, no money, please. It is my duty and an honour." But startled now, he mutters, "Money! My God, do I have enough—for the first year at least?" And as panic almost seizes him for the second time that day, "Will I be allowed to work during the summers? And even if I were allowed, will I find any jobs at all?" And now twisting and turning as he feels himself grow smaller, he sees all around him strange faces smiling and nodding condescendingly with bobbing heads, feels and hears the cold bodies brushing quickly by and shrinking desperately to avoid him, and wonders aloud, "Why was I so cruel to Ma Poppo? I didn't even kiss her properly! And Mildred and Janice too!" feeling hopelessly alone, with hands damp and cold, and forehead moist but hot.

Soon the Viscount, having ended its climb and levelled off, moves onward with more steady throbs beneath the dark-blue dome. And Omoh is much calmer now, as the white fluffs of cloud drift by—not clouds, in fact, but puffs of frosty cotton wool 'flooshing' against the window panes. So comforting! Like a lullaby—a drug that doesn't stupefy. For the children come, and the man in red riding up high upon his horse and singing loudly as he mushes on to find his man and woman too, and the mountains with their massive bullk, and the rivers all aflutter with defiant salmon, and the bears all twelve feet tall and fields of golden grain and—

And now a band of angels swing low sweet chariot coming for to carry—coming for to—coming for—coming . . .

* * *

All this and more Omoh would tell you if he could. Instead, he sits there waiting, no longer staring blankly ahead with tight-folded arms but leaning backwards, lulled into the comfort of deep sleep by fond remembrances. I wish that I could pick him up and put him into bed that he may rest more easily and sleep a long long time and so forget what he knows now but didn't know that morning of his departure from the Rock.

And yet I know and—all too well—I understand that nothing that occurred since his arrival in the big land can ever be erased or nullified. Having lived it once, he must endure it all again repeatedly. And so, he sits there lulled to sleep by the gentle humming of the engines that now heralds the impending landing. He does not hear the plop plop of the wheels emerging from the underbelly of the carrier nor see the fully lowered flaps.

But soon he stirs and hears again, just as faintly as before, "bzz bzz fasten your seat-belts, please extinguish all cigarettes and remain seated until the aircraft comes to a complete stop." Barely awake now, he recognizes the siren voice of the shapely stewardess. Then as he turns towards the window in anticipation of his first glimpse of the big land, sheer terror holds our hero helpless. Some dying monster seems to have wrapped its pale grey shroud around the hovering aircraft! Some huge mysterious creature struggling to remain aloft a few minutes more! For, looking out, he can distinguish nothing—neither land nor sea nor sky. Trying not to panic further, he turns to face his fellow passengers, seeking reassurance. But alas! they too seem to be touched by the grey sickness outside. Only the stewardesses, preoccupied with checking seat-belts, manage hasty smiles.

Fastening his seat belt, Omoh brings his seat erect and sits far back into it. Hands cold and wet with sweat tighten their grip on the narrow arm rests. And Time no longer seems to speed his once-hurrying chariot along. Instead, all motion seems to be arrested, as anxiety grows unbearable and breathing itself becomes a task. In a few moments, however, the Viscount banks far to the right, preparing for its final approach. Omoh, as if to keep his balance, leans far to the left. But soon the aircraft flattens itself out and, holding itself suspended for a few extended minutes, eventually revs its engines up to the necessary speed. Everything is free and weightless now. And there! out of the grey mist (amazing to behold) the runway itself appears, shooting right up as if to greet a lover. The wheels hit heavily, bump several times, then settle down to roll smoothly along the tarmac.

Omoh closes his eyes, breathes deeply in and out, and lets his firm grip on the seat rests come loose. Again he hears the siren voice welcome the passengers to the city of arrival and thank them for travelling by the airline. Then with an extended sigh, she turns off the intercom.

*   *   *

Sitting there before his desk, Omoh seems happy now—in fact, almost excited. Perhaps someone's invisible hand had reached far down within him and set in motion spools of images he had long ago wound up and stored away, causing him to feel again a flury of emotions. For soon, a look of puzzlement appears upon his face. Like a confused projectionist, he seems to be trying hard to stem the rush of images. Perhaps he struggles to black out the more unpleasant ones and to hold still and feed upon the ones he cherishes. Fond hope! for something continues to disturb him.

Indeed, he hears a question asked: "If you could be born again as

10

anyone you choose, who would you like to be? Really, no joke! If you could . . .?" He sees before him eager smiling faces all a-tingle with the zip of tropic life, their smooth ebon bodies masking the healthy blush of childhood, their pale palms sweating within small fists that clench and reclench with knuckles dry-skin white. And once again the question: "If you could be born again as anyone you choose, who would you like to be?" This time, he recognises the well-known faces of the past, some quite dissolved and faded far away into the anonimity of death. And he feels again the flush of mild excitement and tastes the sweet salinity of after-swimming crystals and smells the budding masculinity that reeks from adolescent arms and crotches.

In fact, remembering becomes so vivid that it seems to hold all present functioning of self suspended, there in the presence of the dream-like vacancy of youthful faces tilted skywards, the ratlike rustling of feet upon dry sand, the muffled twack of light back-slapping, the damp rattle of vigorous nose blowing—all these and more. And several voices now much clearer than before:

". . . a millionaire! that's what I'll like to be."

"No man, not me! I wanna be a screen star—like Gable, man. See how all the women and them does go for 'im, all them blondies and them. . . ."

"I don' know, boy, I like me mat'ematics. Could you see me sitting down like Einstein an' writing all them t'eorems?"

"You! ha ha, you and your mat'ematics! who you trying to fool? You can't even add up two and two, so how the hell you goin' . . . ?"

Omoh hears all this like music specially composed and now being played as soft accompaniment to the footage that reels itself out and gathers in loose folds within the confines of his consciousness. And soon, the very images that he himself had conjured up in answer to that question appear—images that he had actually believed to be attainable without being born again: a huge well-polished desk stacked high with books, with inkwells carved out of ancient horns, and pens (more quills than pens) that shape into the written word the visions burning deep within the bearded head that guides the hand that holds them, and manuscripts arranged with neatly matching edges vividly displaying the boldness of the script upon them; a spacious hall with thousands seated underneath large chandeliers, all held completely spellbound by a figure swaying gracefully and urging others seated with scores and instruments to bring to life the dreams, anxieties and triumphs of ancient men with strange-sounding names—and that very figure moving in a flash (or achieving blissful multiplicity) appearing elsewhere, his lightly moving fingers and fast dancing feet stirring ponderous anthems from an awesome looking triple keyboard structure and sending them high up into majestic surgings through slender brazen pipes to move a figure dressed in blue to heightened passion and . . .

But the sheer intensity of reawakened adolescent yearnings now threatens to black out the rerun of the past. Omoh feels himself now lightly afloat upon a soporific tide and sees the air before him come alive with sprightly dancing spots, quite phosphorescent. Staring like a desert traveller who scans miles upon miles of sandy nothingness within the shimmering heat, he tries to summon once again the recent vivid memories. Alas! only a swirl of images run-riot obeys his calls. He tries to hold them still and to perceive the now distorted forms, but without success.

Instead, he hears the question asked again: ". . . if you could be born again as anyone you choose, who would you like to be? Really . . ." and

12

wonders why they, so happy then and feeling so strong within them the glad animal passions of their youth, had indulged themselves in such idle contemplation—why they had dared to limit the happy freedom of daydreaming with such a wild hypothesis.

Ah yes, Omoh sits there now, pondering the question and thinking that, among the aged, such idle speculations would spell out sad recognition of their tragic failures, but surely not among the young, before whom loomed vistas of splendid possibilities. Could there be implicit in such conjecturing a subtle protest against the limitations of our human lot? Or self-immunization against the early symptoms of adulthood? What, if anything? And does it really matter?

But questioning soon subsides, evolving into calm non-thinking, as new images appear—this time from a past more recent. That day, as he lay wakeful on his narrow bed, his head throbbed strangely to a buzzing undertone and his limbs grew heavier with each fleeting second. Suddenly, as if a section of his spring-filled mattress had uncoiled itself, ejecting him jet-pilotlike into the atmosphere, he felt himself jolt bolt upright.

Omoh, you see, had felt himself drop off the edge of waking-sleep and begin to fall (though weightless) into the dark unchartered abyss of sleep. In silent panic, he had roused himself back into the work he knew quite well—so indeed he thought then. Resting on the rumpled covers, he felt quite silly as the tumult of his blood resumed its measured beat. Looking upwards, he fixed his gaze upon a blotch of ceiling, thinking nothing. But soon, a pale kaleidescope of forms appeared on that very spot, rotating in a silent parody of life: pot-bellied infants feebly smiling and grinning bashfully with large empty eyes, twisted bodies of young men bearing unnaturally large joints, young women pre-

dream-like

13 thinking about patients

maturely wrinkled with babies clutching in vain at large breasts gone flat with hunger, several dust-covered figures too aged to brush the flies away abandoned in protracted dying, an amputee (much too young for that) striding defiantly along a path tapped out with white-tipped cane—and many more, rotating slowly then faster and faster still, then speeding up into one constant blur of rapid motion.

But see! Omoh slumps forward on his desk now, quite shaken and exhausted. Perhaps we should let him rest awhile, for he has suffered much. Not just those things he recently recalled and lived again, but many others. I know that he would want to tell it all to you. But since he sits there silent and still shaken by the aftermath of reawakened feelings, let me fill you in.

* * *

PART THREE
A Story

Therefore, my dear friend and companion, if you should think me
somewhat sparing of my narrative on my first setting out,—bear
with me,— and let me go on, and tell my story my own way:—or if
I should seem now and then to trifle upon the road,—or should
sometimes put on a fool's cap with a bell to it, for a moment or two
as we pass along,—don't fly off,—but rather courteously give me
credit for a little more wisdom than appears upon the outside;—and
as we jog on, either laugh with me, or at me, or in short, do
anything,—only keep your temper.

Laurence Sterne

"So this is the big land," Omoh sighed, his nose crushed against the frosted glass. Rain, falling not heavily as in a tropic downpour but steadily, had for a long time now been trying to wash the dark clouds from the skies. "Then and only then," he thought, "would I be able to see the distant mountain tops—even the precious sun perhaps."

"Let's go, we must register today, despite the rain," a voice of wisdom advised from a nearby doorway. "It has been spitting for a few days now and may continue for a long time yet."

Already the old grey army huts, assembled in the semblance of a hamlet, were spewing forth well-coated, unbrella-protected bodies that splashed about with galoshed shoes.

"My, what big feet these people have," Omoh observed. "But no faces! just so many heads tucked turtle-like deep within so many turned-up raincoats."

But he recalled that he too had splashed clumsily along through pools of water on the day of his arrival, wetting shoes and pant cuffs. Reluctantly he walked out into the rain, as he had done so many times since his arrival. And as he moved along, he recalled the details of that very day.

Once the aircraft had landed safely, Omoh's fellow passengers, having escaped the grey sickness of the skies, had put on their hats and coats. Each one, anxious to pursue his individual goal, became his old accustomed self again, completely insulated from the others and the world around.

Omoh, dressed in a light tropical suit, joined the file of bumping bodies walking up the aisle. As he approached the stewardess standing at the exit, he turned to catch her eyes, then muttered similingly,

"Thank you for a good flight," then, more lyrically, "Goodbye for now, dear, hope we meet again some day."

Without taking notice of the objects she offered to him, he rushed out onto the ramp. But only to rush frantically back into the shelter of the aircraft! Standing there, arms clasped about his shoulders, he was completely oblivious to the angry stares of those passengers against whom he had rudely bumped. But soon he began to understand his plight. Thinking of island sunshine, he had quite forgotten the pilot's weather report. In any case, he could not understand why he should feel so cold on a fifty-degree September day. My God, what would he do when the winter truly arrived!

Just then, much to his relief, he heard the siren voice addressing him,

"Here Sir, courtesy of the airline."

Somewhat abashed, he turned to see her holding out in his direction

16

a light raincoat and an umbrella.

"See," she added, almost cooing now, "we meet again much more sooner than you thought."

Grinning sheepishly, he put on the coat with her assistance, moved once more onto the ramp and opened the umbrella, then still shivering lightly, walked out into the rain. But as he walked, he suddenly felt alone and quite afraid. With each step his feet grew heavier. Looking disconsolately downwards, he saw that both his shoes and even his pant cuffs were soaked. Indeed, he had just stepped into another pool of water that had been hidden by a blur of tears.

Soon uncomfortably wet feet raised themselves up onto a platform and then came to a full stop. Automatically, Omoh shut the dripping umbrella and entered a huge building. Stirred by the warmth within, he felt new courage rise tingling through his veins. "Thank you very much," he chirped to an airline employee standing nearby, as he returned the borrowed articles, then moved on in search of his luggage.

Eventually, Omoh stumbled into the arrival lounge with an over-stuffed suitcase—all the more conspicuous because of its bright red colour—bumping against his bony knees at every step. Pausing, he let the suitcase fall heavily to the floor as new doubts carved furrows upon his shining forehead. What if Johnny had forgotten to meet him!

No longer tingling with new-found courage, Omoh felt his socks slip further down into his sodden shoes. To think that he had met Johnny not quite a year ago! But it was he who had encouraged him to save his money, to make the necessary applications and leave the Rock for the big land. What a blessing true friendship was. And there! almost too good to be true, was Johnny, standing between two boys he did not know. Thank God for good friends. Wish there were more like Johnny.

Quickly grabbing up his suitcase, Omoh hustled towards the welcoming trio, wiping away a solitary tear that threatened to betray his sentimentality and thinking all the while that he had not really kissed Ma Poppo good-bye, nor Janice, nor Mildred.

Now, two weeks later, smiling as he recalled such things, Omoh walked on to register. He remembered how quickly the dampness of the rain-drenched day had been dispelled once he spotted Johnny and his friends.

"How's the folks back home?" he heard Johnny inquire.

"Quite well, when I last saw them," he quickly responded.

"Your mother's quite a woman," Johnny continued.

"The best there is."

17

And soon the drive back to the campus had begun. Questions were asked and answers given freely and eagerly.

"So how's the weather down south, Omoh?"

"Why, marvellous as usual, maybe even a little too damn hot."

"Too hot! Just wait a few months, my friend, you'll understand that it's never too damn hot."

"The fog? Oh, that's been around for some time now. But don't worry, you'll get accustomed to it."

"Hey man, brought up any good rum with you?"

"Sure, you think I'll leave my medicine behind?"

"Ha ha, ha ha ha."

"Any good parties up this way?"

"Why, things have been really swinging the last few weeks. In fact, there should be a good one Saturday night."

"Well, that's good."

"Not so sure I'm going, through."

"Why not?"

"Boy, the woman who giving this one put out lots of fellas the last time. She likes to pick and choose."

"Tell me, how were jobs this summer."

"Jobs? Well a few people, like my friend Johnny, made a mint."

"And the others?"

"They managed to survive and even to stack away a bit."

"Really!"

"Yes man, but tell me more about the Rock, man."

Calm with mild optimism, Omoh had spoken freely. And as they swished along the fast-flooding streets and avenues, he watched many things of interest go by. But most of all, he took notice of the bridges. So many bridges were there! What a feat of engineering to yoke together a land, so strangely broken up, into one unit—into a city obviously quite young, but thriving and expanding rapidly. And so beautiful indeed! But alas! Omoh had seen no mountains nor great rivers as yet. No matter though, he thought, in time they would appear—magnificient as ever.

And still exulting in such confidence, Omoh trudged on to register. He no longer felt the dripping of the rain nor the dampness of his feet. For the very notion of becoming a *bona fide* member of such a noble institution as the university filled him with the warmth of pride—even as it had done two weeks ago on his arrival on the campus. That evening, he had been assigned to temporary quarters—a pleasant and spacious room, evidently meant for two. So thrilled was he, though tired, that he had failed to notice (or had unconsciously neglected to do so)

18

the drab exterior of the campus buildings.

And later that very day, he had also recognized among the many faces in the dining hall the unmistakable features of an old acquaintance. Happy and excited, he had found even the tepid soapy-tasting sausages and the not-quite-baked potatoes palatable. In fact, nothing could have dismayed him then—not even the non-smiling middle-aged stout women dressed in white who served the meals, nor the long bare tables arranged in martial order, nor the mess-hall atmosphere. Not for one moment did he miss the warm informality of family-eating back home. Nor had he come close to suspecting that that early evening meal, light as it was, would always be the heaviest of the day—so very much unlike the various types of ground provisions, tightly kneaded dumplings, well-stirred corn coo-coo or some such solid foods that were piled highest on noon-day plates back on the Rock.

* * *

That day of registration, Omoh walked home, six hours after standing in a rain-drenched line. He knew that there would be no bright sun in an hour's time to warm him, as there would have been back home. The streets were wet but clean—in fact, much cleaner than the many ones he had walked back in his island past. Yet they were not happy, they did not speak of life—of song and dance and madness.

As he stepped cautiously through the puddles—for he still had no overshoes—the confused sounds of happenings earlier that day droned loudly in his mind. In vain, he tried to shut them out, feeling wet and tired. But the monotony of voices persisted unrelentingly.

"Your faculty? . . . courses approved? . . . by whom? Well then, proceed over to the other building, please."

"What! you left your cards behind? . . . too bad, you must go back for them . . . next please."

"Oh no, you, back into the line again! now fill the booklet out . . . all twenty pages of it too."

And so for the second time that day, Omoh confronted the perversity of the day's arrangements, wondering once more why anyone should have to sit for pictures not early in the morning when fresh and nicely groomed, but later on after tedious hours in hot sweaty rooms, and thinking once again that those in charge (whoever they may be) must be real sadists!

And at that very moment an image of himself escaped-convict-like appeared, with eyes that usually protruded fish-like now fully sunken deep within the prominent forehead, with long pointed chin and sharply jutting cheekbones threatening to pierce the thin skin that glistened with a clammy moistness, with tie partially undone and hanging limply from the neck, with shirt collar wide open to relieve the fiercely projecting Adam's apple and with jacket, already over-padded to disguise the narrow shoulders, drooping at an awkward angle from sloping shoulders.

Just then, however, a sudden angry squeal of tires quite shattered the unhappy image of himself. A car, flashing red lights tracing broken circles from its top, jerked to a stop beside him. Two tall men quickly emerged—cold-looking men with boy scout hats and lanyards, pale khaki tunics, dark pants with thin yellow stripes tucked neatly into shining clean brown boots that reached high up their legs.

They did not sing! Instead the sterner of the two, an officer apparently like Nelson Eddie but quite unlike him otherwise, spoke with a croak but quite politely.

"Young man, you've just jay-walked, you are now liable to fines of no less than twenty dollars."

"Wha—! Who? Me?" Omoh heard a strangely high-pitched voice inquire.

"Yes, you son, you've just jay-walked."

Frozen with fear, Omoh stared fixedly at the face before him and felt his limbs loosen and his bowels dangerously tense in sheer confusion. He hardly realized that he had crossed the street and, even if he had, he would not have understood that he had erred—in the stern eyes of the law, that is. And so he stood there staring limp and wet, and wondering just what the hell jay-walking meant.

"You've crossed the street illegally, my friend," he heard the voice explain, as if in answer to an unspoken question—and even more politely now.

No less perturbed, Omoh managed to explain that he had just recently arrived into the big land that was far away from his little Rock where he was born, and had not had a chance as yet to become familiar with the many laws here.

Still not smiling Nelson-Eddie-wise, the two officers consulted for a while and decided to press no charges at this time. But not before the voice had warned,

"But just you remember this, young man, ignorance of the law is no excuse. Good day."

A wetter, colder, sadder, wiser man, Omoh finally escaped. Walking all alone, he then remembered that he had not kissed Ma Poppo properly, nor either of the girls, on that day of his departure.

***

when he gets depressed he thinks of home.

20

Two months later Omoh lay in bed, listening intently as the weatherman announced the possibility of a light snowfall early the next day. It was much cooler then, but the rain had fallen almost constantly. Darkness came much earlier and the sun rose later. Omoh had not yet seen the snowflakes fall, nor had he heard the new snow yield crunchingly beneath his tingling feet, nor felt the feathered dampness brush against his cheek, nor smelled the quickening freshness of a snow-filled day. And so the thrill of anticipation ran through his body, already warmed by two blankets and most efficient radiators. Turning over onto his back, Omoh pondered the mysteries of the weather's gradual change. Indeed, he had not forgotten how completely he had been made a fool by the summer's prolonged daylight.

It was the day after his arrival when he had gone to cricket practice— not so much a cricket practice as a social gathering for the purpose of discussing the past week's happenings. The rain had temporarily stopped and the temperature had risen slightly.

A few zealous contestants hurled vicious-rising, short-pitched balls at a few ambitious batsmen, trying hard to keep their places on the Varsity eleven. Occasionally too, some fleet-footed fieldsman would chase a well-hit ball across the field. Yet sprawled right there upon the grass within the boundary-line a large contingent of supposed onlookers, critics and even a few permanent members of the team (the somewhat bow-legged captain included!) listened eagerly as elegantly attired Sir Free presented dramatic renderings of the most recent party's highlights.

At intervals laughter, loud and raucous but happy and spontaneous, would drown out the feeble knock knock of cricket balls upon the bats. Sometimes too, some member of the audience, a participant in the drama of the party-night, obviously perturbed in anticipation of impending revelations, would grow restless. And soon all eyes, deftly guided by the right forefinger of Sir Free, would turn in the direction of the guilty person.

Alas! that well-known forefinger! so awkwardly bent at the first joint and so ostensibly innocuous. That right forefinger by which Omoh himself was destined to soon be pointed out and held transfixed, squirming and withering slowly. Unlucky victims, who several times that day had themselves enjoyed a hearty laugh at someone else's expense, would wince repeatedly as Sir Free's well-aimed remarks hit home.

Sitting on the grass that day amidst the others, Omoh had felt a warm glow of comradeship well up inside him—a sensation quite similar to that which he had felt the day before, during the drive to the *daylight Saving 1 hour.*

campus. He felt—in fact, he knew for certain—that everything would be all right. Had he not met a few among the campus crowd that he had known back home? Surely, there would be no loneliness here. Indeed, Omoh had already begun to share the ardour of life at university—something that could only grow with time.

So completely engrossed in dreams about the future was he that he did not notice the group beginning to split up. A few boys, however, amateur dancers and drummers, came over and invited him to watch their show at a downtown club that night. And so they decided to part for a short while until they met later at the Blue Skies. Big Jay would pick him up at ten o'clock sharp.

Still exhausted by long hours of travelling the day before, Omoh decided to sleep for a little while, before getting himself ready for his first look at night life in the big land.

No sooner, however, had he made himself comfortable in bed than he heard unmistakable tootings of a horn just outside his window. Surely they were not meant to summon him, for Big Jay had said ten o'clock, and they had just been playing cricket. Time could not have flown that fast.

But then the sound of heavy knuckles knocking on his door brought Omoh scrambling out of bed. Jerking the door wide open, he almost bumped into Big Jay, whose amazingly wide grin displayed a set of perfect teeth, sparkling white and bright—a striking contrast to his dark smooth skin. Upon his upper lip a most unusual moustache, unkempt and quite uneven, threatened to run wild.

Big Jay's attire was equally unique. He wore a shining black long-sleeved shirt, rust-coloured corduroy pants held up by a broad, bright red leather belt with a huge brass buckle, bright yellow socks and light brown desert boots. His car, a fifth-hand pale blue Nash, stretching itself out torpedo-like, with seats that folded backwards to form a spacious sleeping place, stood almost in the centre of the narrow roadway—the pride of many months of diligent car-lot research.

"But you are a hell-of-a-man, man! You ain't ready yet?" Big Jay exclaimed, hardly opening his mouth or moving his lips. His voice, quite naturally loud, achieved a greater resonance with each word.

Completely stunned by the sudden onrush of events, Omoh just managed to mutter, almost stuttering, "A-a-I thought you said a-a-ten o'clock. And so—"

"So wha'time you think it is now?" barked Big Jay, making his way further into the room. Despite the harshness of his voice, the broad grin fixed upon his face seemed to reassure all who met him that he was the happiest, most spontaneous, and friendliest person one could get to known. In fact, as Omoh was soon to learn, Big Jay was quite a delicate young man. So much so that he carefully avoided all contact sports. The body, as he himself put it, was too precious to be subjected to such brutality. He had to keep the merchandise intact!

"It's just after ten now," he heard Big Jay announce.

"Buh-but I don't understand. We were playing cricket just a while ago."

"So what difference does that make? It's summertime you know, my boy," Big Jay continued, "the fish are jumping downtown and this ain't no time to slumber. So you better hurry up and get yourself dressed."

What Omoh soon realized was the cricket practice had ended at nine o'clock! Big Jay indeed had arrived at ten o'clock.

Snuggling up more closely to his pillows, as he recalled such things, Omoh realized that he had already become a veteran of downtown nightlife. He heard the dark green radiators, recently reactivated, gurgling softly as rust-coloured water flowed through, bringing much appreciated warmth from the tired boilers. The still-hot air, tainted with the mustiness of blankets rescued not long ago from summer storage, threatened to become oppressive. But the lure of reminiscence held him fascinated.

He remembered how, a long time ago, he had been introduced to the phenomenon of seasonal changes. With the aid of multi-coloured globes and maps and blackboard illustrations, he had been repeatedly shown how the lengths of days and nights around the world varied and changed as the earth rotated and revolved around the sun. But one of those lessons so carefully learned had come alive before his very eyes. And he had failed to recognize it at the time! How could that happen, especially to one who had always excelled in geography!

The drive downtown, he also recalled, had been in no way disappointing. Big Jay, long shapely legs (for Big Jay was a devoted though seldom triumphant athlete) stretched comfortably out from the driver's seat already pushed back as far as possible, kept up a constant rattle of small talk. The big blue Nash, rolling and swaying torpedo-like, seemed to pursue a course it knew quite well.

Still flashing his sparklingly happy smile, Big Jay spoke of his many experiences downtown, at the same time supplying Omoh with all the necessary briefings.

"Look, Omoh," he began, "when you get to the club you have to put that bottle underneath the table—on a little shelf built into it for that same purpose."

"What! You mean I have to hide it?"

"Yes indeed."

23

"From the moochers?"

"From the boys in blue." [police]

"You mean to say that it's illegal to drink booze in the clubs?"

"Right on, my friend. Actually, the men are not so bad. But the women cops! You got to watch out for them. If there's a bottle on the floor, don't reach for it or else they're shaking hands with you and charging you at the same time."

"My God! good thing you told me that. You know we can drink freely any place back home—outside, inside, on the streets, on the beach, anywhere we choose."

"You don't really have to worry much down here. Even when the boys get mad and decide to stage a raid, the peeper at the doorway spots them coming and flashes a sign, gives you lots of time to dispose of the evidence."

Obviously enjoying his role, Big Jay spoke of many other things— about the bouncers ever-anxious to preserve the establishment's good name yet sufficiently kind-hearted to double as bootleggers, about the regular girls most eager to make a stranger's night on the town unforgettable (as Dinah Washington would put it), about the dances introduced by visiting Blacks who, often too anxious to enjoy the privileges of a more polite society than the one they knew down south, woke up next morning to discover disturbing aftermaths, about the floor shows featuring second-rate pop singers—one-time Ed Sullivan performers fleeing the struggle for survival in the entertainment jungle further south, about the strippers engaged in acrobatic feats that were quite skillful but also titillating or twirling brightly coloured tassels miraculously fitted onto firm-nippled breasts, about the dope addicts staring with glazed eyes right past the ecstasies of life they hoped to find when high—about many other things.

Soon the big blue Nash rolled to a stop and they anxiously emerged, but right into the full blast of a voice shouting in fierce contention with an orchestra that seemed about to drown it out each minute. As if some Circe had whispered soft seductions in his ear, Omoh stood transfixed with one hand resting lightly on the open car door. Any minute then he half expected to hear a snap, a gurgle and a gasp—and the voice go dead. But the shouting, harsh but strangely fascinating, continued relentlessly. Through the many cracks and crevices of the old building it poured. Through a tiny well-concealed peephole at which an aged man with dirty-looking unkempt beard kept constant watch, it rolled, vanquishing whatever other sounds of urban life unfortunately crossed its path.

But soon the voice, sufficiently triumphant, ended its shouting and went silent, for a few seconds at least, until a whining guitar solo proclaimed a follow-up performance, this time with obvious efforts to achieve a softer, warmer tone.

Only then did Omoh realize that he had climbed the steep stairway. A sharp buzzer, announcing to the doorman the presence of two new paid customers, spoiled the Circe's magic. Immediately the door, guided by a massive forearm covered all over with tattoos of the deep-deepest blue, snapped open, allowing them to enter.

Omoh, who had once dreamed of wearing the perfect body-according-to-Charles Atlas, gazed for a while at the still-extended arm. That arm that had hurled so many bodies limp with drink bumping painfully down the stairs to the pavement below! That arm that to maintain a safe and happy atmosphere for the loyal patrons would smite with crunching impact the hardiest forehead of the most raving drunk or brave the most frantic slashings of some hopelessly frustrated pervert!

"We-ee-l boys, yee can have this table 'ere. I'll send the others over soon 's they gits 'ere."

Vaguely aware that he was being spoken to, Omoh felt himself being gently propelled into the allotted seat. Within the poorly ventilated room, dense gatherings of smoke hung cumulus-like rendering already dim light from low-powered coloured bulbs a lurid grey. The heavy air reeked of tobacco and of urine, of stale drinks and of sweating human parts.

For a moment, Omoh seemed about to faint, but the scene he saw beyond a blur of tears that bathed his smarting eyes quite fascinated him, off-setting the physical discomfort. Vague remembrances of night-clubs on the Gaza Strip back home came to his mind. But this was something else!

"The show's over, time for action now, miboy," Big Jay eventually exclaimed, carefully lifting his huge self from the uncomfortably small seat.

The band, obviously worn out by the frenzied tempo that had climaxed the strippers' torrid dance, left the stage for a short break. The other performers had all withdrawn to the privacy of small rooms at the rear left of the hall—not so much rooms as closet-like recesses. The doorman, meanwhile, proceeded (with deft movements) to fold up the rope which had cordoned off the magic world of stage. Without the slightest warning, the brightest of the lights put themselves out and the jukebox, restored to life, blared out the final twenty bars or so of a top hit that had been abruptly cut short when the show had started.

"It's jukebox time, miboy. The band will soon be back, so let's case the joint."

Guided by the then-familiar voice, Omoh followed Big Jay across the room. A few couples had already made their way onto the dance floor. Like victims of some vengeful Furies, they leaped and jerked, gyrating rhythmically in strange ritualistic fashion.

Staring incredulously, Omoh felt his spirits drop quite low. Had he not boasted to Big Jay on the way downtown that he had been "one of the best" on the dance floors back home! Had he not assured him, furthermore, that his musical know-how would enable him to overcome whatever difficulties the new dances may pose! And now this! How could he ever venture on that floor tonight? What's more, he had been looking forward to the occasion with great anticipation.

Already the band seemed to be getting ready to return to the stage. Big Jay, who had hustled over to meet the others who had just arrived, was passing on the details of his scouting to them. And soon they all had settled down, as the old-talk flowed free and loud.

Omoh, for a while, forgot his fears. Besides, he had quickly downed two or three extra-long drinks of Scotch, thinking, "Wish there was some good Vat around," and too, "You know, maybe if I dance the slow ones first, I could get a feel for them—then later on, maybe I could risk the faster ones."

At that moment, however, the band began to beat out the quick rhythm of the Genius' number one hit. All the other boys moved out in search of partners. But Omoh remained seated, hoping to add a few more ounces of bottled courage to his system before chancing the ordeal.

But alas! right there, approaching with a broad display of sparkling white teet, came Big Jay with two buxom young women in tow. Hastily Omoh gulped down his half-emptied glass, almost choking in the process. He heard himself being introduced.

"Well girls, this is Omoh, fresh from the Rock, a great guy and a fantasteek dancer too!"

Omoh's cheeks grew hot, his tongue seemed stuck in his mouth, already dry with apprehension. Rising to meet his new acquaintances, he sagged dangerously at the knees. But he held himself steady against the table, forced a smile on to his bony cheeks and extended his hands to greet his fair ladies, remembering all the while that he had not kissed Ma Poppo! Nor Mildred nor Janice!

Big Jay winked slyly at him and, with unexpected clarity, announced, "This is May and this is Angie, the best in the whole damn house."

"Hi girls," Omoh answered weakly, completely startled by his own voice.

"Well, what are we waiting for?" inquired Big Jay. "Leh's go, baby," he slurred, returning to a more familir intonation.

Blinking rapidly, Omoh watched as his friend led May onto the dance floor to join the mass of fast-gyrating bodies. Almost in a daze he followed, leading Angie by the hand he had not let go since the introduction.

Soon like a cornered animal, he turns to face the inescapable. Angie, meanwhile, has freed her hand and already begun to respond to the driving tempo. Like a pagan priestess lost in the ecstasy of hallowed rites, she writhes and turns and twists before her hapless partner. Flawlessly, she moves through her routine, one so modern yet so well-preserved from pagan days by her ancestors. Pulling himself together, Omoh begins to do the steps he knows quite well. Dancing his very best, he moves gracefully in true island-fashion.

But in a few minutes, after bumping heavily into several other couples, Omoh realizes that he is the odd-man-out. What would have been a superb performance elsewhere at some other time was now completely out of place.

Angie, sensing his predicament, tries to lessen his embarrassment by slowing down, but he tries harder yet to match her steps—with disastrous results. The band, inspired by the ecstic dancers, plays long and hard. Omoh feels sick. Everywhere he turns, pale ghost-like faces leer at him, asphyxiating him. The stage the lights the table—everything spins crazily about the room. Any minute now, he would fall down.

Just then (almost miraculously!) the music lost its voice, the dancers stopped their movements and the floor emptied itself, spilling the tired couples off to the sides. Angie, who seemed to have realized that Omoh was an accomplished dancer but just unfamiliar with the popular routine, led him to his seat. With each step, she gave his hand a gentle squeeze of reassurance.

But Omoh did not respond—in fact, he did not feel a thing! he knew full well that he would soon experience (for the first time in the big land) a barrage of teasing, such as he had witnessed on the cricket field earlier that day.

And true enough, no sooner had he sat down beside Angie (who seemed to have become a member of the group) than Big Jay, so recently his friend and kind adviser, began the assault. Alas! so completely unnerving (but yet so amicable) was it all!

"Boy, did you see ole twinkle toes tripping into action? Jus' like me ole man! Hoy Omoh, tell me mahn, was that the Charleston or the Turkey Trot? You know you should 'ave been on the blimy floor show! Ha ha ha. D' you realize . . . ."

Omoh no longer listened—in fact, he no longer heard the voices, thinking that at least he had escaped the dreaded venom of Sir Free's forefinger. Letting his head fall wearily upon the wooden backrest, he sought some refuge in the aura of the lady he had temporarily forgotten. Her one hand still clung to his, the other gently mopping his forehead with a tiny handkerchief.

Inhaling the warm incense that emanated from it, Omoh felt his head grow lighter, as if he had been drugged. Then new but more familiar visions appeared before him—soft sunlight, salt sea breezes, calm waters far and wide, heavily laden coconut trees swaying gently, darkly smiling faces—

But then! what rude hand now tries to pluck him from his newfound haven? He would not give in. What harsh voice calls him Orpheus-like back to that other world of din and smell? He would not follow it.

No rude hand indeed nor harsh voice either. Just Angie firmly shaking him and calling urgently, "Omoh! Omoh! wake up! Your friends seem to be getting into some kind of trouble."

Omoh then realized that he had fallen asleep, temporarily done in by drink, exhaustion and (most of all) chagrin. The babble of voices had ceased, but a deep drawl persisted:

"Ah'm asking yuhawl again, what language d'yuh boys speak? Ahn' down't gi'mee that bull-sheet thah yuh speaking Eengleesh, darn eet."

Indeed, the tongue that spoke was weighted down with excess of drink. The group, knowingly silent, smiled at one another. The question, though heard by all, remained unanswered.

"Yuhawl mus' be Coobans, that's eet," the drawl continued. "Mus' be Spaneesh yuhawl speaking, eh Carstro?" it queried, lunging in the direction of Big Jay.

Somewhat befuddled by the situation to which he had awakened, Omoh tried to make quick sense of it, thinking: that fellow must be drunk and looking for some noise. What could he hope to achieve against so many—despite his blubber? Surely no one among us is a coward—in fact, he himself had been in many a tough spot before. But would any of the other natives of the big land, who are now looking on in interest, come to the support of their white brother in distress? And moreover, even if the boys manage to hold their own against the crowd, what about the repercussions? The police, the courts, the newpapers, disciplinary action by the university, the scandal back home! Why must life be so difficult? Can't a guy just have some innocent fun? Back on the Rock that bastard wouldn't dare provoke a fight. He would be pulverized! Especially—

28

"Ahnswer me! or ah'll smash yuh gawdarn Carstro face!" the drawl resumed, becoming dangerously more belligerent.

Big Jay, at whom the threat had been directly levelled, took firmer hold upon the almost empty bottle underneath the table, hoping that he would not have to waste the precious stuff, but confident of the support of his fellow islanders. Moreover, he was determined to protect his delicate but beautiful physique from any harm.

Omoh, fired up with loyalty, banished all fears and doubts. His tropical blood, not yet cooled down by North winds, throbbed violently in his veins. After all, his good friend was in danger! Besides, there was Angie looking on with interest, apparently quite concerned about his safety! And there was an opportunity to make up for his earlier performance on the dance floor! Indeed, he must show the others that he too was made of sterner stuff and so win a rightful place within the group, the Vice Squad, as he later discovered they had been dubbed by the less adventurous.

Jumping to his feet, Omoh made straight for the still threatening drawl, intending to strike the first and only blow. And this he would have done had Angie's restraining hands not caught hold of his shirttails. Yelling at the top of his voice, he struggled to escape—or so it seemed—oblivious of all dangers.

Fortunately for Omoh, the bouncer with the massive arms quickly approached the scene, calling out quite casually, "Now look'ee 'ere my man, you're drunk. Time to be on your way home to beddy bies now. Be a good li'lle boy now, you hear me."

Omoh, abruptly cutting short the remarks he had been hurling at his opponent, stood paralysed. Could the Fates be that cruel, indeed? Must he be put to shame a second time this very night? And within such a short space of time! And with his lady there beside him!

"Now look'ee'ere, my man," the massive arm repeated, "These boys been comin' 'ere a long time now. And they don't bother nobody. So cool it, baby. Watch it, mother," sounding almost lyrical.

Realizing then and only then that the words of caution were meant not for him but for his opponent, Omoh sat down slowly, sighing with obvious relief.

But then the drawl retorted, "Aw g'wan you. Take care or ah'll smash yuh gawdarn face een."

That threat so bravely made was not to be fulfilled. Looking upwards, the blubbery drawl saw for the first time the stern face that looked down upon him. Besides, the massive arms that bulged out from the tight shirt-sleeves spoke their silent piece.

With a nervous chuckle, he suddenly inquired, "Whah's wrong

weeth yuh felluhs any'ows? Cahn't yuhawl take a li'lle joke?'' and adding, to the surprise of everyone, "Have a dreenk on me, come awn now.''

As if by sleight of hand, a twenty-six of Scotch appeared on the table with a thump from the inner pocket of his coat. The bouncer, apparently satisfied that he had made his point, withdrew to his station at the door. But the boys had had enough to drink and rose to leave. Besides, how could they share a drink with such disgusting blubber!

But the drawl insisted, breaking the seal right there. Big Jay and Omoh, wishing to escape the situation, decided to accept the offer. With practised skill, each put the full bottle to his mouth and tossed it back, swallowing an unusually large amount of drink. The others, suddenly experiencing a change of heart, followed suit. Soon they hurried to the door, leaving the drawl to contemplate his almost empty bottle and holding back the laughter that would erupt once they left the premises. Before they made their exit, however, they made sure to thank the bouncer for his kind assistance.

Turning to Angie who had walked him to the door, Omoh smiled at her, noticing for the first time that she was quite attractive.

"See ya soon, m'dear," he whispered softly in her ear, letting his lips brush lightly across her right cheek, from which a thick coat of makeup had long ago rubbed off onto his shirt.

"Sorry it had to be like this the very first time we met," he added in all earnestness.

Leaving her standing there somewhat bemused, Omoh proudly shook the massive hand, muttering "Thank you," then walked out into the cool night air. He was tired but exhilarated too. True enough, he had made a complete jackass of himself and had been put to shame and taunted for it. But wasn't that a fit initiation to the clan? Surely, he would not behave like that ever again. And besides, no one had made mention of the fatal dance since the more recent incident—not even once! Surely he had been admitted to the squad by silent acclamation.

Sitting crushed between two stronger bigger bodies in the back seat of the big blue Nash, Omoh no longer felt cold. Shutting his eyes, he surrendered himself to the peace of calm contentment. And then came sleep, deep sleep, like a drug— only it doesn't stupefy. And a band of angels coming swing low sweet chariot, coming for to carry—coming for to—coming for—coming . . .

* * *

30

Still lying in bed, Omoh gradually discerned the confused goings-on of early morning resident activity. In the near distance, slamming doors recoiled upon hinges powerfully sprung and others whined in loud protests as ghoulish faces pushed their way reluctantly out into the dampness. Occasionally, a brief silence! as some rumpled face peering out from beneath a tangled mass of hair paused to contemplate the sullen out-of-doors. With bleary eyes unwashed and blinking idiotlike, he held the door ajar as if in disbelief—yet knowing all too well that what he then beheld was what he expected to be there.

Just then, as if he had been goosed by a well-practised finger, Omoh sprang out of bed, tossing on to the floor the limp sheet and the prickly blankets that had kept him warm. It had just dawned on him that he had overstayed this mark. In fact, he knew that he would have to rush to make his lecture on time, so powerful had been the drug of reminiscence earlier that morning.

Whispering curses to himself, Omoh hurriedly performed the rituals of ablution at the communal wash-basin. Soon back in his room, he observed within the familiar mosaic that was his mirror a countenance that stared at him—a countenance quite pale and hungry-looking, but not dangerous! They faced each other for a while in silent contemplation. But soon the tarnished image reshaped itself into a smile of unexpected radiance.

"My God!" the smiling form exclaimed in unspoken words. "It's supposed to snow today, the weatherman predicted that it would, on the late news last night."

Unconsciously the rhythm of brushstrokes quickened, as eager anticipation of the unknown seemed to breathe new life into the frail body. A bird-like whistling further betrayed the excitement that he felt.

A few minutes later Omoh dashed out of the building, headed for his lecture. That morning he had spontaneously resolved that he would not gulp down the clammy cold oatmeal, nor would he choke upon the scrambled eggs spread sparingly upon soggy toast. Today he would ignore the cook's magnificent obsession.

But then, a sudden shower stopped him cold! Alas! this could not be. Rain drops! not really raindrops, but blobs of crushed-up ice spattering directly against his face. And then, a direct hit upon his neck sent a curious trickle running down beneath the collar of his shirt and all along the hollow of his back—or rather, where the hollow should be—into the nether regions.

"How horrible!" he thought aloud, squirming as he began to run. "How can this be? Where now the feathered lightness of the 'flooshing' snow-flakes? Where now the softly crunching snow yielding to the impress of lightly treading feet? What grey presence, shedding large and mushy tears, dares to falsify the confident predictions of a trained professional and disappoint the public? How could the elements themselves so flaunt their power in the face of one of nature's most ardent lovers, by twisting the preordained design of day beyond all recognition?"

Omoh could find no solace anywhere. The cold November winds, indifferent to his empty questionings, shrieked their shrill symphonies through the thick-leaved evergreens along the roadway. And then, to show that Nature too could be outdone, a student car that hustled its pooled forces on to punctuality threw up a wave of slush beside him. So accurately did it find its mark that Omoh would have sworn that it had been directly aimed at him, had he not known how courteous and polite those natives were.

Had he no so far been addressed as "Sir" and "Mister" by each and every one who publicly attended to him! And besides, so many persons had come to him, quite unsolicited, and chatted cordially with him!

"Do you like the weather in this province? The very best in all of the big land, you know!"

"What made you choose the lovely West coast, my boy?"

"Where do you come from, son? . . . Mmm-mm-m, now where is that? Ah yes, Africa. No? Oh! Well well, the West Indies! Oh well."

"Is your Queen still as fat and radiant as she was when she rode triumphantly in an open car during the coronation ceremonies— despite the heavy downpour? Yeah, your Queen, we just loved her. . . What! Really? That's who she was? The Queen of Tonga. Why, of course, how silly of me."

"My friend, what is your native language? You speak English so beautifully! . . . Really? All your life? In such a tiny island? Now isn't that fantastic? Hip hip hooray! Jolly good, ole man. God bless the Queen! Long live the Queen! May Brittania always rule the waves— and islands too."

Omoh, in fact, had been specially selected by a Rotary-sponsored international group to enjoy the privilege of a Christmas dinner with a rather important member of the community. And just imagine! all four generations of the family would be represented there. Besides, a few chosen friends had been invited to share in the exotic evening!

Already, Omoh, a rare gem in a land of treasure-hunters, had achieved celebrity. Why should he dwell unseen within old shoddy buildings? Better to blush quite visibly in the warmth and comfort of a lavish suburban living room.

* * *

32

Somehow Omoh managed to arrive at the lecture room on time. Cold and wet and completely disillusioned, he hurried to find a vacant seat before the rest of the crowd got there.

At least, he consoled himself, all was not lost. Where Nature did betray the heart that loved her (despite Wordsworthian guarantees) and bared her teeth and claws, one might still find fair haven within the portals of the intellect.

A sharp buzzer sounded the half-hour and the professor entered promptly. On sagging shoulders, he wore a loosely-hanging, faded black gown, moth-eaten and heavy with many years of accumulated chalk-dust—a symbol of academic triumph long gone stale. Sitting wearily upon his chair, he turned the well-worn pages within the yellowed folder to a marker just recently put there. Then he began to read his lecture. In fact, he almost spoke by rote the words that he had so carefully composed a long time ago.

As he spoke, he often lifted up his head and cocked it slightly so as to display a patch of greying hair he proudly wore. A titter of excitement fluttered through the room as full-breasted girls, blushing as if somewhat ashamed of their well-rounded beauty, responded to the proximity of masculine maturity and wisdom. Stimulated by the elixir of female adoration, the paragon of intellect assumed his well-known stance behind his desk. With chest full out and shoulders squared in military fashion, the veteran spoke out with growing confidence.

At first Omoh listened carefully, intent on taking copious notes. But as the lecture steadily rolled on, spinning a perfect web of boredom, his eyes grew tired. In fact, he soon became increasingly oblivious to the shapely figures round about, who by that time had been reduced to various attitudes of vacant awkwardness. His clothes, still wet and cold, clung tightly to him in jealous ownership, his stomach growled repeatedly in fierce demand.

And soon, his mind betrayed him too. The lecturer, his tired shoulders drooped once more and chest withdrawn into its accustomed hollow, no longer pontificated. The calm assurance with which he had begun had faded fast, leaving instead a hint of mild embarassment. But the voice relentlessly played out its dull monotone—a fitting counterpart to the dull plop plop of ice against the glass-paned walls.

Turning his head to the left, Omoh twisted his body in the opposite direction, seeking greater comfort. The wooden structure, bench and desk held firmly together by an iron frame, offered little relief to his thinly fleshed behind. In an effort to relax, he tried to think of nothing. And soon succumbing to the hypnotic voice, he felt his limbs go loose. A look of calm repose settled upon his face. Indeed, he seemed quite happy then.

For then the frosty fluffs 'flooshed' frequently upon the roofs, the children's happy shouts did not disturb him, nor did the loud singing of the man in red high upon his horse, the awesome mountains and the rivers silently approved, and the grain-filled fields nodded their assent.

No dried tubers there, no red rock with carrion mouth, no empty thunder nor ghostly sounding winds. Just sleep, deep sleep—like a drug that doesn't stupefy, and chariots dangling softly tinkling bells—how sweet! coming for to carry—coming for—coming . . .

Just then, however, no tinkling bells but a harsh and grating buzzer shattering that other world of winter. The dull monotone resolved itself into a sigh of great relief. The folder snapped shut upon its marker, already moved on a little further. The personage, his dusky coat then gathered tightly around his body—but not sevenfold—descended from his pedestal and joined the rush out through the doors to find a fix of tepid campus coffee.

Startled by the irritating buzzer, Omoh banged his knees sharply against the iron framework of his desk. Anxious to avoid the curious glances of the others, he pushed his way on through the crowd with unusual roughness, seeking anonymity. But soon he felt himself being carried along by the flow of addicted coffee drinkers towards the fast-approaching cafeteria.

Back home, Omoh had been too busy doing other things to discover the luxury of daily coffee drinking. Since his arrival in the big land, no one among the natives had offered to initiate him into the secrets of the ritual. Besides, he could hardly spare a dime.

And so, at the last moment, Omoh avoided the cafeteria, thinking that he should perhaps visit the house for foreign students instead. But he was in no mood for table-tennis nor card playing, nor for light bantering nor (worst of all!) for the intellectual exchanges that were so persistently encouraged.

Finally goaded by the prickings of his instincts, he turned abruptly and walked toward the residences. In fact, he had not written home for quite some time, and so he could spend the day responding to unanswered letters and writing to those he had so far neglected. Thinking such things, he pulled his neck deep down into his sweater turtle-like (as he had seen the others do) and walked briskly on, quite heedless of the day's unhappy conditions.

* * *

34

Another day, the sun looked out admiringly upon the young city, already sprawling far and wide beneath it. Along the many streets and avenues, the pace of life, considerably slackened during the colder, more damp days, had once again begun to quicken. Even the land itself seemed to enjoy the pleasant weather that had recently arrived and still prevailed.

A lone helicopter, hovering lazily under a brilliant sun, seemed to contemplate the scenes it witnessed below. The frisky shoppers anxious to exploit the many after-season bargains, the eager salesmen hoping to detect prospective buyers, the curious visitors in search of souvenirs, the students of all ages conscious of the fast-approaching holidays, the casual strollers out for no other reason than to enjoy the balmy atmosphere—all these and more, apparently oblivious to the actual time of year, were dressed almost as if it were a spring day.

The headlines of the local dailies, meanwhile, boldly and somewhat gloatingly spoke of record-breaking snowfalls in the prairie provinces and of lower temperatures much further to the east.

And out in the distant west, the coastal range displayed its massive outlines. The mountains, awesome in stature, stretched out their rigid bulk in calm repose, their profiles softened by the thick coverings of snow. A few blemishes here and there revealed the spots where men, fleeing the dull routine of urban life, had left behind the traces of their rapid zigzags down the gentler slopes. Protected by those lofty sentinels, the irradiant waters of the gulf beneath quivered invitingly, unconsciously disguising the bitter cold within whose grasp they lay. The adjacent land, apparent veteran of some ancient and mysterious violence, proudly exhibited the many man-made braces that held it all together. Reaching far up between its multi-fractured bulk to greet the icy waters of the rivers, the sea appeared to soothe those pains that happened to persist. The spacious parks, the city's vital oases, enjoyed a greenery most unusual at this time of year in other regions of the big land. Two other spots stood out, however, like scars upon the land. Not so much scars residual from accidents of by-gone days, as wounds inflicted recently upon the healthy landscape where enterprising families, with government assistance, had dared to carve out new suburbs to the north and west.

Within that panorama, a city bus rolled on at moderate speed, taking its load of tired bodies back home from the city centre. Up front within that bus, a lonely figure, somewhat preoccupied, sat gazing at the passing world outside. Just then the frail form, jerked forward by a sudden stop, scrambled awkwardly back into his seat. And there he watched new faces enter and pass by the empty seat beside him, on into the

when sitting on a bus alone w/ room to spare beside + no one takes it

fairly crowded bus.

But Omoh hesitated to look back lest his suspicions be confirmed. Glancing slyly to his left, however, he checked to see if by some chance he might have occupied more than his portion of the double seat. And almost instinctively, he drew himself more tightly up against the window.

At the next stop, more people entered and once again passed by the vacant seat. Omoh knew for sure then that every other seat was occupied. Why should this be happening? he asked himself. Was he not decently attired? Could he have been mistaken for someone of no good reputation? Or could there be some natural preference for travelling at the back of buses? Very strange indeed. He then recalled that day just after his arrival when an aged woman had chosen to remain standing rather than accept the seat he offered her.

Despite a strong gut feeling, Omoh avoided what seemed to be obvious conclusions. Those things could only happen in the Deep South, he persuaded himself. The people of the big land, as all the world well knew, were courteous—and polite! To them, all men had been created equal—except perhaps the once-savage (but later completely tamed) people whom they had placed on reservations and who (as he had heard from students at the university) stubbornly refused to help themselves.

Besides, he was a member of the Commonwealth! And too, a student at the university who could hold his own against the average person on the bus.

Just then, as the bus veered sharply to the right, Omoh realized how close to the window he had been sitting. Somewhat puzzled, he began to wonder why he had behaved like that. Of whom was he afraid? And why should he be worried if others chose to make themselves uncomfortable? Especially if, by so doing, they allowed him special luxuries!

And so, with a look of triumph beaming on his face, Omoh let himself relax, stretching his legs well out and sprawling in full ease. Pleased with himself, but somewhat fascinated by his own reaction, he felt new courage stir within him. From then on, he resolved, he would remember to enjoy the advantages which apparent handicaps promoted.

But deep down inside, Omoh knew that he had little reason to be self satisified. In fact, the reality of his financial position soon undid his proud composure. The last month had been most eventful. Not only had he moved into a new home off campus, he had also written his first formal examination and spent his first Christmas away from home.

* * *

It all began one chilly morning when Omoh, emerging from the dining hall, walked lazily across the grounds to the office of the residence to collect his mail. Unfortunately, there was none. Only a little slip of yellow paper on which was written in a neat hand, "Please call at the main office."

Anxious to discover what was wrong, Omoh hurried to the room next door. Right there before him, a head, completely bald and quite pink, teetered toy-like upon a short and much too slender neck. Five stubby fingers, yellow-stained from years of nicotine contamination, drummed out strange rhythmic patterns on a desk. The other five, just dimly visible behind a cloud of smoke, were loosely clenched around a stout cigar that glowed beneath its ashen top.

"Good morning, son," the pink smile beamed. "What can I do for you today?"

The genial voice seemed to dispel the gloom that hung around. The many fears that had assaulted Omoh upon discovery of the note were much allayed. Affected by the buoyancy of spirit, Omoh returned the friendly greeting, flashed a far less fleshy smile and revealed the yellow slip of paper.

"Good morning to you, Sir. I found this in my mail slot and decided to come right over for the good news."

"Ah yes!" exclaimed the pink head, as it bounced forward unexpectedly, and stubby fingers grasped the note.

Soon those very fingers expertly flipped through a stack of papers, yellowing them somewhat. Then they plucked out a single one. And once again, the head rolled backward precariously upon its slender pivot. The face continued to smile, but the voice that spoke had suddenly become imperious.

"Within three days, you must remove your belongings from the room you now occupy and take them to number 16A of the camp a little further down the road," the toy-king ordered. "Your room has been reassigned to graduate students arriving a little late from overseas. The camp is neat and fairly comfortable. A little further off indeed, but not too far for young legs like yours," he further explained.

Had it not been so early in the morning, Omoh would have sworn that he detected whiffs of alcohol escaping from the mouth that addressed him. But the head, as if exhausted from holding itself straight up, resumed its original position. The briefly dispelled atmosphere of gloom gathered again as Omoh turned to leave. The weight of all his recent problems seemed to have doubled and redoubled.

Not only was he seriously perturbed about his swiftly dwindling finances, not only was he still disgruntled with the disappointing weather, not only was he already unhappy with the meals and most other aspects of life in residence, but he was severely racked with anxiety over approaching examinations.

Much more important, moreover, Omoh had begun (for the first time in his life) to feel quite lonely. Surely, he had established close relationships since his term began—that is, besides his older acquaintances. But it was a peculiar loneliness! a loneliness—in fact, a yearning for warmth and tenderness such as he had previously enjoyed with Janice and Mildred (whom he had not kissed), compounded by a disturbing uncertainty of what Christmas would be like away from home and Ma Poppo (whom he also had not kissed on the day of his departure).

Just as he was about to talk through the doorway, he heard the voice again.

"By the way, I almost forgot to tell you, you will be sharing your room with another student from—"

"But do I know him?" Omoh instinctively inquired, interrupting it.

". . . a third year engineering student," the voice resumed its statement. "He owns a few pieces of electrical equipment, but there should be no problems anyhow. You boys from them islands mostly travel light."

Omoh did not respond. Instead, as if infected by the bobbing disease, he nodded slowly, then let the door slam shut behind him. And before he fully realized it, he was well on his way to the camp that was destined to become his home. In a short while, he arrived in front of the group of army huts that had survived both world wars. Since it was Saturday, the residences were very much deserted, for most of the students who lived not too far away had gone home to visit for the last time before the end of term.

Omoh cautiously moved to the stairs that would take him to the section called the "A" huts. The environment was bleak, the quiet quite disturbing. No dining hall here! No recreation room! To enjoy such facilities, he obviously would have to make his way back to the other residences.

Finally resolved to face the worst, Omoh ran up the short stairway, pushed the outer double-door open and walked slowly to the door marked number 16. When several sharp raps received no answer, he cautiously tried the lock and, much to his surprise, the door creaked wide open.

Had someone chanced to pass by at that very moment, one would have marvelled at the frail figure, almost grey-complexioned, standing there holding the door open, his already large eyes bulging fish-like from their sockets, his mouth as if arrested in the middle of a shout and his knees wobbly as if about to buckle beneath his light weight. But one would have soon also seen that very figure, like a would-be burglar surprised at his first job by a gun-toting master of the house, launch himself into a wild dash out into the open and, without stumbling once, not come to a halt until the unconditioned body screamed out in agony of sheer exhaustion.

At that point, Omoh let his panting self bend over, hands upon knees, striving all the while to slow down the rhythm of his breathing, lest the frail heart should give way to the strongly thumping blood. And soon enough, the painful distention of his narrow chest subsided. With some effort, he then straightened himself up on reluctant knees.

Mad at himself, he shook his head repeatedly and continued (walking then) along the main boulevard. Occasionally, he furtively glanced backward to see if by some freak chance someone might have been pursuing him. How then, he wondered, would he explain his rather strange behaviour?

Meanwhile, the details that had so recently impressed themselves upon his startled mind during those brief moments of note-taking returned, more vivid then in calmer recollection: a room just barely more than half the size of the one he occupied, a bunk-bed double-decked—the bottom part already claimed, a small table tightly squeezed into one corner fit for no more than one person's use at any one time, the other corner piled high with electrical equipment of all sorts, a tiny window to the right above the table protected by discoloured wire netting that grudgingly would allow a small breath of air to seep through.

Omoh desperately hoped that perhaps he had visited the wrong room. Or perhaps there could have been some error made at the office itself. Surely that room could not be shared! Then why the double-bed? he argued with himself.

Standing there on the open roadway, Omoh (for the second time that day) suffered an attack of claustrophobia. Despite the chilly atmosphere, several spots of perspiration appeared upon his forehead. Cold shudders rippled up and down along his spine and a tightness pressed in against his rib cage. Instinctively, he wrapped his arms in firm embrace about himself, as if he were cuddling new life into some poor infant abandoned by its destitute young mother.

And so he might have stayed for some time had not a car come lurching around a nearby curve. Startled by its sudden appearance, Omoh pulled himself together and walked forward, trying to assume a look of equanimity. But then he saw behind the wheel a familiar figure flashing its accustomed smile, revealing sparkling white teeth beneath a tangled foliage of moustache. The car itself was none other than the big blue Nash he knew so well. Immediately, he felt that Big Jay and his Nash were happy omens. Yet he feared that he would somehow betray his recent emotional upheaval. For Big Jay would certainly deride him for being such a sissy.

Moving over to the curb, Omoh watched the big blue car bear down on him and, with a squeal a groan and a sigh, come to a welcome stop beside him.

"So what's happening deh?" he heard the familiar greeting.

"Nothing much, man," he quickly responded, trying to be calm. But already Big Jay's smile had gathered itself into an expression of concern, for he had perceived that Omoh was not his usual self.

"Eh eh, like you just got some bad news," he observed. "Anything serious? Something's wrong back home?" he queried.

"What!" Omoh weakly exclaimed, with an effort of a smile. "Nah man, just taking a walk. Like everyone's gone home for the last weekend before exams," he continued.

"Come in the car, nah man," Big Jay invited him, at the same time pushing the door open. His voice seemed to have lost its well-meaning raspiness.

Omoh, in whom strict upbringing had engendered a kind of phobia for dishonesty, could no longer hide the truth. And so, letting himself sink into the spacious seat beside Big Jay, he related the story of his experiences earlier that morning, omitting only the details of emotion he could not put into words. But before he could tell it all, Big Jay had started up the big car and sent it rolling along an alternate route off campus. Omoh, in fact, had only just completed his description of room 16A when the big blue Nash affectionately rubbed its tires against a curb it seemed familiar with and crawled to a stop before an old three-storey house, partially screened by evergreens.

Somewhat perplexed by Big Jay's apparent indifference, Omoh watched as Big Jay opened the car door and started to get out, wondering just what he was supposed to do.

"What's wrong, man?" the strangely softened voice intruded upon his thoughts. "Aren't you coming with me? Just dropping in on an old buddy of mine for a little while."

"I wasn't sure—" Omoh began to explain, but soon thought better of it.

Instead, he followed Big Jay out of the car, around the right side of the building, down into a dark basement and towards an awkward-fitting door, on which a hand-written sign warned, "ENTER AT YOUR OWN RISK."

40

With only a single sharp rap to announce his presence, Big Jay pushed open the door and bellowed, "Wake up, my man. You goin' to sleep your life away?" Without stopping, he made his way into an adjoining room.

Overwhelmed by the swift and unexpected development of events, Omoh remained standing just inside the door. Emanating from a frying pan that bubbled vigorously with what seemed to be chicken being cooked the island way, a once-familiar smell filled the room. Already he could feel responsive glands begin to salivate.

Just then, he heard a squeaking of the tired bed-springs upon which Big Jay had just plumped himself down. And then a thwack, a yelp and a crack of laughter, splintering all around the inner room and spilling through the door to where he stood.

"But you are a hell-of-a-man, man, dropping off to sleep in the middle of cooking," he heard Big Jay reprimand his friend. "You want to start a fire or what?"

The voices, however, soon softened considerably—enough, at least, to prevent Omoh from hearing what was being said. Left alone and still unsure of just what was going on, Omoh sat himself down upon a well-worn couch fitted tightly into the space just opposite the range. There he could feel the desire to partake of the soon-to-be-eaten meal grow stronger with each minute. And soon a thin mist began to blur his moistening eyes, as the nostalgia that had been affecting him so often recently hit home again—this time much stronger than any time before.

The quick emergence of Big Jay and his friend, however, forestalled any developments that might have been embarrassing.

"Kopakie, meet my friend, Omoh, another member of the Vice Squad," he heard himself being introduced.

"Hi fellah," Kopakie's silken voice chirped lyrically as Omoh rose to greet him.

"Not so bad, Kopakie," Omoh blurted out, feeling the warmth of the two hands that now enclosed his.

"Take off your coat and sit down, man. Make yourself at home," the silken voice advised him.

By that time, Big Jay had already reached far into a small cupboard in search of something. Soon brandishing a half-filled bottle, he inquired, "Too early for a little touch?"

Considering the time of day, Omoh was just about to politely refuse the offer of what was obviously strong drink, when he recognized the label.

"Vat! Vat 19! I can't believe it!" he heard himself exclaim instead, as he got up to admire the elixir he had not seen since his own stock had run out.

"See what I told you, Kopakie, a man after my own heart," Big Jay observed.

Somewhat abashed, Omoh turned and resumed his position on the couch as a burst of happy laughter flooded the room, arousing goose pimples all over his arms and legs.

"So what's this I hear? Old wobble-head trying to evict you?"

Taken aback by Kopakie's unexpected questioning, Omoh managed to reply, "It looks that way, indeed", at the same time accepting a healthy slug of Vat that Big Jay literally forced into his hand.

"Cheers! and down the hatch!" Big Jay proposed and promptly swallowed his entire portion.

Omoh had forgotten how strong the stuff actually was. Shocked by the silent explosion in his throat, he almost yielded to the urge to spit it all out. But he dared not risk losing his fast-growing reputation. And so, with bulging Adam's apple working feverishly, he downed the precious drink, hoping all the while that the others wouldn't notice the blurring of his eyes. But soon the blurring threatened to send tears rolling down his cheeks—this time not because of explosive stimulants nor memories of home, but on account of unbounded gratitude. In fact, Omoh still could not believe what he had just heard. Kopakie had invited him to share his home with him—if and whenever he so desired. And more! he had invited him to have some stewed chicken, peas and rice and avocado pear.

***

"Arbutus!"

The bus driver's voice roused Omoh from his reverie. A good thing, indeed, for he must make ready to get off at the next stop. Looking slowly around, he discovered that there were few besides him on the bus.

When he eventually stepped down to the pavement, he smoothed the creases of his pants as he was wont to do. Walking down the quiet street, he inhaled the freshness of the mild sunny day deep into himself. His feet touched lightly on the ground as he literally bounced along. The houses themselves, with their Christmas decorations still not taken down, seemed to radiate the cheer of a season well enjoyed. Summer chairs and tables, unmoved since the last year, stood upon healthy-looking lawns. A few young ones, not bundled up but clad in spring-like outfits, hurled fast balls at an unmasked catcher.

A little more than halfway home, Omoh decided to take a brisk walk down to the beach, which was still washed by wintry waters. Soon seated on a log beneath the evergreens which hung over the secluded cove, he began to feel a coolness he considered more typical of the area. The log itself was damp, though far from the water's edge. And so he moved out from the shade, seeking a spot more directly open to the sun's rays.

Pondering the subtle changes of temperature that he had experienced, he picked his way among the rocks. So chilly in the shade but quite warm in the open! Had he finally discovered the wisdom of Ma Poppo's favourite observation, at which he always smiled in fond contempt? How often had he heard her say, "My my, but the sun's hot today," and thought to himself, "How could the sun be anything but hot?" Smiling again (though not as skeptical), he then recalled the many aphorisms he had heard her utter, remembering too how frequently he had discovered the wisdom of her words—but much too late!

Omoh leaned against a tall rock, careful to avoid the many jags that threatened to destroy his trousers—one of the too few pairs he owned. In the distance, a ferryboat sailed on leisurely, reflecting the sunlight that fell upon it. How smoothly and effortlessly it moved upon the waters of the inlet! He would give anything to be aboard right then. Especially since he had not yet visited the islands off the coast.

"Boy," thought Omoh, "how different it would be from those other trips across the Bocas from one island to the other," reflecting on the more trying moments he had experienced at sea. Especially those while travelling on the Blue Liner—no bigger than a rich man's yacht, but much less efficient! To think the government had risked so many lives by hiring such ships to make so dangerous a crossing.

But Omoh was in no mood to contemplate the problems of his country. Turning his head slowly from left to right, he let his eyes trace out the distant coastline, thinking aloud, "City centre would be a little farther to the right and further inland. What a beautiful place—when the sun's out, that is. Boy, am I ever glad I chose to come out to the coast. Imagine living somewhere without the sea nearby! I would go crazy. Mmm-mm-m, it's so good to sit and watch the wide expanse of water and let your thoughts roam aimlessly wherever they may choose. Here everything makes sense, or perhaps it is that all problems, personal or otherwise, become unimportant. Here nothing matters but the quiet and the beauty, the rhythm and the harmony you see and feel. How good to lose all sense of time, to quite forget the self and to be absorbed into an existence that means something, though difficult to put in words. Here one—"

But sudden recollection cut short meditation. Up to that moment, Omoh had forgotten that he had promised to go downtown with Big Jay

And so he must return home and get a rest before the appointed hour.

But musing recommenced as the word "home" ran through his mind. For, to him then, home meant a small basement apartment off campus. What a lucky break it had been for him to get that place. No palace by any means, but a warm home. He could never thank Big Jay enough. Nor Kopakie. What great guys those two had proved themselves to be. Thank God for good friends.

And starting for home, Omoh wondered why he had not kissed Ma Poppo on the day of his departure. And Mildred and Janice too.

He keeps thinking about this

*   *   *

Seated on the couch, which would become his bed at night, Omoh forced off his shoes and stretched his legs full out before him. Clasping his hands loosely behind his neck, he slowly reclined and let his eyes fall shut. The lingering smell of recently cooked, highly seasoned meals reminded him that he had not yet eaten anything that day. Still he postponed the idea of preparing something, preferring instead to ease his tired limbs a while. But shortly, heavily treading boots thudded up then down the tired stairs out front. A single throb within his narrow rib cage pained his heart, and then his pulse in sympathy sped up its beat. And too his eyes responded, forcing eyelids far apart. But otherwise, his attitude of apparent calm remained.

Omoh's first urgings were to rush upstairs to see what letters had arrived—to see whether indeed the anxiously awaited grades had been released. But apprehension held him still. What if they really were upstairs? Where would he find the nerve to tear open the envelope, take out the folded contents and read the information that was recorded there? Supposing he had failed to live up to his expectations! What then? Where would he ever find the courage to write the necessary supplementaries? What would he say to the family and many friends back home?

Instinctively, he sought the warmth and comfort of his own embrace, rubbing his feet quite vigorously one against the other as a strange chill ran through them. How could he possibly have failed, especially since he had not once been stumped by any of the questions? Except perhaps he had been guilty of repeated oversights! Omoh indeed was satisfied with each of his performances, even believing (though no regretting) that he might have over-extended himself the last few weeks of preparation. Moreover, he had too often worried himself sick unnecessarily those days. So simple were the questions. Actually, the examinations were not much different from those he had written in college back home.

Often, indeed, they were much easier—especially in the case of Latin, the pride and joy of island-educators.

True enough, studying in the apartment had not been easy. The light had been inadequate, for he could not afford a reading lamp like the one Kopakie owned. The dingy radiators could not compete with their more efficient counterparts back in the residences. And the dropping of the temperatures at nights had often forced him to put on another suit of clothes over his pyjamas while he studied. Quite often too, he had resorted to the little warmth that flickered from the small three-burner gas stove near the couch. The little pliers that were needed to turn on and off the worn-down controls were always handy nearby on the shelf.

But on the other hand, he had escaped the crowded dining halls where he often studied on the campus. No longer did the frequent opening and shutting of noisy doors make concentration difficult. Nor the constant shuffling of restless feet, nor the scattered whisperings of less devoted ones, nor the more distant sounds of traffic just outside. In his small apartment room, he enjoyed a quiet that he knew only when he had shut himself up within his campus quarters—but without the solitude.

Kopakie, a three year veteran of examination writing, had studied close by in the other room. Omoh indeed had envied him his calm, methodical approach. So often had Kopakie's unexpected bursts of song, late at night, eased Omoh's anxious feelings. So often too had Kopakie's soft voice calling out to him in friendly chit-chat provided a most welcome pause. In fact, on one or two occasions when studying was impossible, they had joined in (or rather, themselves helped to organize) impromptu trips downtown to catch a late late show. Omoh never minded that, as long as he had revised the past day's work and read the sections of the texts that would be discussed the next day. Besides, he never missed a day at class for he considered regular attendance to be half the preparation for exams.

Just then, a voice! a woman's voice, aged and quite unsteady, called out to him, "Mail's here, Omoh."

Miss Banard, owner of the building, had always shared the concerns of the several students who rented rooms from her. So, like some gallant to the rescue, Omoh responded to her call, oblivious of all dangers. Jumping off the couch and rushing through the door into the dark basement and up along the inside stairway, he eagerly received the five envelopes handed to him by the pale and twisted figure whose eyes gleamed gleefuly.

"I hope it's all good news, son. I know how hard you boys have worked," Miss Banard wished him well.

A middle-aged spinster, she stood upon the stairway at halfway point. Her thin hands, as if immersed in soap suds, seemed to be engaged in washing each other free of some unsightly stain. The ungainly movements of her thin crooked fingers betrayed a slight deformity, adjusted to through years of painful effort. Besides, she held her narrow shoulders much too high. And yet, as always, she displayed a cheerfulness and charm that years of suffering had failed to taint.

So many times had Omoh listened to her explain her preference for students from the islands.

"You boys are all such gentlemen," she would say, "so warm, polite and honest. And you get along so well together, almost as if you knew each other long before you came here." Then with a somewhat mischievous smile, she would add, "But Freddie's my favourite. He's like a son to me. Now don't any of you get jealous. He first knocked on my door in answer to a sign I scrawled on my door."

No wonder Omoh wished that her one big dream would soon come to pass. He hoped that she would one day find the means to leave that chilly land (so unsuitable for her) and seek the hot and sunny lands of South America. Especially Columbia, her earthly paradise. There, he believed, she could pursue, with greater comfort, the travels through the realms of literature she so dearly loved.

That day, her glistening eyes revealed the zest for life that glowed within the pallid body—a zest for life that seemed so alien to even the most robust natives of the big land. Almost trembling with expectations, Miss Banard regarded Omoh standing there before her with the letters in one hand, the other, tightly clenched, freely bedewed itself as it rested on the staircase. He, meanwhile, realized that she had recognized the official envelope and longed to hear her confidence in him confirmed.

As if he were a robot guided by impulses beamed from those eyes that held him fixed, Omoh briefly contemplated the little bundle, selected one of the two official envelopes, slowly tore it open, then read its contents. And soon he offered the neatly folded piece of paper to the anxious woman, then let himself sink gradually onto the step on which he stood. And then, that voice again! this time much less uncertain but much more high-pitched with joy.

"I knew it, I knew you'd do it. I told you so. I'm so proud of you, my son. A first class mark in literature. Indeed!"

Omoh, in fact, had done quite well. The one second class he had received was high enough to preserve his first class average. But his fears—just overcome—dissolved themselves into a solitary tear which he allowed to trickle down his cheek quite unashamedly. Pulling himself up, he reached out and shook the withered hand that had been extended to him in all sincerity, at the same time saying, "I'm glad I didn't let you down."

"I know you're anxious to pass on the good news, Omoh," Miss Banard responded, "but don't forget to come upstairs some time soon and have a glass of sherry with me."

With that, she turned and slowly made her way up to the second floor, leaving Omoh free to retire to his room. For he must share his happiness with everyone—especially those back home. First, he would make the necessary phone calls, then write the necessary letters. Boy-oh-boy, how good to be able to life one's head in proud defiance of all those who dared to criticize his friendship with "that crowd—the Vice Squad, we call them." But he must not let success go to his head. He must remember to strive for even better results in the finals later on. Perhaps he should soon start to read the next term's texts quite soon.

Turning around, he hurried downstairs, wishing once again that there was something he could do to hasten Miss Banard's departure for the tropics. What had she done, he wondered, to merit such a fate? Why had she been damned from birth to suffer such deformities? Why such unjust atonement for the sins of her father and mother—if indeed they had sinned that badly? If not, what other reason was there for such suffering enforced upon a woman with such a good heart?

Unable to find answers to such questions, Omoh threw himself upon the couch once more. He felt the elation of his recent success rapidly subsiding. Quickly he shut his eyes in a desperate effort to blot out the image of suffering that hovered genielike before them.

Omoh himself had been quite frail, but he had never once been fragile. Nor had he suffered any noticeable loss of health—except for the usual childhood ailments, such as measles, mumps and whooping cough. And these, ironically, had rendered him immune from further attacks of the same diseases. And yet, he then recalled, like some pouting schoolboy who had not been allowed to have his way, he had so often complained about his lot in life and sulkingly withdrawn himself from the company of others. In striking contrast to such conduct, he remembered once again the pale but happy countenance so recently before him—a countenance so full of cheer and gratitude, of love and expectation.

A sharp touch of guilt made Omoh wince uncomfortably. He felt quite small and relatively weak. Still obviously experiencing the thrill of personal success, he could not banish from his mind the disturbing reality of man's uncertain destiny.

With a sudden sweeping of his arms, as if to drive away the unpleasant visions that haunted him, he lunged from the couch and rushed into the next room—Kopakie's sacred domain. Reaching into his back pocket, he pulled out the little red book in which he kept the few numbers he had so far collected. After several diallings received no answers, he stood staring at the brass knobs of the antique bedstead.

Returning dejectedly to the outer room, he sat once again on the couch. The lingering smell of highly seasoned food no longer stirred his glands. No thoughts of hunger moved him then. His eyes stared glossily across the room, his arms hung loosely at his sides, his open palms turned upwards as if begging alms.

And soon upon the brown doorknob on which his eyes were focussed, the images within his mind projected themselves in a rotating kaleidoscope and then merged into a blur of rapid motion, to the accompaniment of a whirring sound. The loosely hanging arms swung into motion, clamping hands firmly upon his ears, while eyes surrendered to the blur's hypnotic motion.

Suddenly, the spinning stopped, the blur faded completely, the whirring sounds grew silent, and the brown door knob resumed its familiar form. Gathering himself together, Omoh looked apprehensively about the room. In vain, he tried to contemplate the recent vision and to comprehend it. Instead he felt a dizziness, such as one experienced after turning round and round for several minutes.

Flattening himself out upon the couch, Omoh sighed aloud, thinking, "Gee, if only I could find someone to tell the good news to. If only Ma Poppo were here, or Mildred, or Janice."

But unfortunately, none of his friends had been home to receive his call. Ma Poppo, Janice and Mildred were much too far away. Too far to share his joy immediately, to drive the dizzy feelings off, to make him feel the swell of life rise up within him. If only they were there to talk with him and touch him and so generate that something without which life degenerated into a slough of doubts and fears, into a jungle thick with intellectual snags, into a haze of meaningless existence. If only they were there with him, then he could kiss and feel the tingling and the issuing forth of self that made his being real.

But all alone! What indeed could one frail individual do to combat those inexplicable forces that so often seemed to thwart one? How could one, all by oneself, appreciate the meaning of success or assimilate the happiness that comes with it?

Yet, though alone, he must not soften. Nor should he allow himself to slump into despair. Especially since there were reasons enough to celebrate! For to deny the smallest part of self-fulfilment was tan-

48

tamount to self-abuse. He must keep that in mind. For the time being, however, he would seek a brief respite—just for a few minutes.

And as if in answer to a prayer well heard (though quite unspoken), Omoh felt himself slip slowly off into the neutral world of sleep. Such a pleasant feeling! So vital to one's well-being! But, as they say, so much like death!

A shudder ran coldly down his spine—a horrible sensation. And then, before his eyes squeezed tight to shut the daylight out, dull dark red spangles danced sequin-like, fascinating him. And soon, the dancing ceased and the darkness grew much thicker. Breathing became more regular—more audible too, somewhat hypnotic. His head, then twice its weight, sank deeper and deeper into the corner of the couch—a corner already quite sunken by the frequency of similar occurences. His limbs went strangely limp. As if controlled by puppet-strings, legs folded up and in against thighs and knees moved higher up into the hollow of stomach, arms bent compass-like upon the fulcrum of elbows pulled themselves down and in to fill the space left, while hands clasped loosely into double fist fitted themselves snuggly into the curve of neck. Upon his face fully relaxed in sleep, a look of calm self-contentment displayed itself—a countenance that vividly reflected a child-like innocence.

* * *

A wide expanse of flat grassy land rose gradually on all sides into a little hill on which a thick-leaved tree of medium height stood mushroom-like and all alone. Not far above, small clouds puffed up in ruffled whiteness flounced along like chubby Chinese wool-dogs at play. Flooded with liquid sunlight, the sky much further up exhibited a deeper shade of blue than it was wont to wear. From distant shores, warm breezes romped inland bestrewing a freshness in the air. And in the air, a host of birds, unrecognizable amidst the dark-green foliage of the solitary tree atop the hill, warbled a curious harmony of sound in soft andante.

Floating lazily upon a firm but gentle gust of air, Omoh looked about quite casually, but obviously enchanted. Soon he felt himself being wafted slowly downwards on to a thick green cushion of grass beneath

49

him. But suddenly the gust seemed spent and he began to fall free. Not speedily nor with feelings of discomfort or premonitions of impending danger, but easily—almost weightlessly. Somewhat like an astronaut with no umbilical cord to guide him safely back to mother-ship. Then like a proficient sky-diver slowed down by television cameras for stunned onlookers, he rolled twice over, head first, then landed with light bounces upon the grassy rug.

Picking himself up, Omoh moved with long high-bounding strides on to the hillock there before him, as if he were guided by some Ariel-sprite. He saw no flowers there, no butterflies. In fact, no signs of other life appeared.

And then beneath the tree, he heard (much louder then before, but still quite soft) the harmony of chirps and cheeps, of trills and twitters—the strains of unseen birds. Entranced, he sat down, quite slowly letting his back slide easily along the soft smooth tree-trunk. There upon the grassy cushion, he scanned the dark-green surface that seemed to undulate right on to the distant horizon.

"This is the life," he thinks. "No irkings of the mind here, no achings of the heart. No ups and downs—just calm peaceful self-contentment. Perfect happiness, never to be disturbed."

But soon, the harmony of sounds begins to cloy, the breezes lose their erstwhile freshness. His entire self grows heavy, sinking slowly down in to a green mushiness that threatens to engulf him. The surface of the land then heaves itself into huge grey billows that rumble ominously.

Omoh feels quite helpless—incredibly inept. All efforts to cry out prove to be futile. Besides, to whom could he cry out for help? There is no other person here to hear him. His so recent paradise has become a

50

hell! And so unexpectedly!

Just when existence seems no longer possible (no longer desirable, in fact), a soft voice whispers to him. Omoh looks up and, much to his surprise, beholds right there a fair creature angellike who reaches out to him and takes him by his outstretched hand. And off! He feels himself being borne aloft out of the hellish sludge. Shutting his eyes to savour his relief more deeply, he sighs aloud. And then he opens them and looks around to gaze upon his fair saviour once again. But she is gone! Alas!

Instead, he hears a door shut softly. Rude hands take hold of him and draw him upwards and then let go. Aghast, he clutches desperately at the empty air, moaning soft words. And then, the sound of laughter from afar!

What evil spirits mock him so? He must strike back regardless of the consequences. And so he strikes out blindly and furiously at the gloating demons, intent on rescuing his fair lady and saviour too. Alas! a sharp pain numbs the arm that finds its mark.

"What the hell!" he cries out, grasping the elbow that still throbs with pain. Raising himself to an incline upon the other elbow, he blinks repeatedly to wipe away the fog that has arisen. Then gradually, he perceives a vague form that somehow seems familiar. And he hears an equally familiar voice.

"Wake up, ole man! it's time to go. We've got to celebrate."

Omoh, though much more awake then, could not understand that he had slept so long. Five o'clock! Impossible. But then there was Kopakie home from a long day's working at the lab. Somehow though, he didn't seem to be as tired as he usually was at that time. Sitting fully upright, Omoh watched him to a bump-and-grind into the next room.

Then he realized that Kopakie, like himself, had received good news. But he also felt a strange discomfort which he immediately investigated.

"My God!" he whispered to himself, "not in broad daylight!"

Grabbing his trouser-front to check the flood that threatened to expose him, Omoh rushed headlong out into the tiny basement lavatory (constructed in deliberate defiance of city-zoning ordinances). Once there, he searched to see if any wetness had oozed through and left revealing marks. Satisfied that he had managed to avert all chances of detection, he returned to his room in time to hear Kopakie explaining that Big Jay would pick them up in a few minutes. Then after a good feed at the Chinese nearby, they would pay a casual visit to Sir Free, who had just received some stock from home. Finally, they would proceed to a most fitting climax (the only thinkable one, in fact) downtown.

Startled by Kopakie's innocent choice of words, Omoh sniggered and hurried to prepare himself for the day's adventures.

* * *

The big blue Nash rolled slowly but confidently on to the restaurant where Chinese dinners for three or more persons could be had at special student rates. Completely relaxed in the back seat amidst a scattering of training equipment (for Big Jay was still a most devoted athlete, though not successful), Omoh allowed reflection on the day's events to take its course. But he could not quite understand the nature of the questions that had earlier perturbed him.

Familiar scenery passed by as he pondered the apparent mystery of it all. To think that it had happened so unexpectedly. And at such a peculiar time too—when his spirits should have been soaring sky-high.

And then that dream! Omoh chuckled to himself but soon remembered the presence of others, from whom the incident must be kept a total secret. So concerned about that was he that he furtively looked down to reassure himself—despite the fact that he had changed his trousers. How could that have happened? Never since his adolescence

52

had such a thing occured. Nor had he been thinking of any special woman at that time—consciously, that is. Perhaps, he smilingly surmised, that was Nature's way of counteracting his frustrations. Indeed, he had not once enjoyed the ecstasy of sexual intimacy since his departure from the Rock. So completely wrapped up in reflection was Omoh that he just barely realized that he was being spoken to by Big Jay.

". . . is Curly doing. Mo ole man? Making any progress there?"

"Not really," Omoh managed to answer somewhat spontaneously.

"M'boy's playing it cool," Kopakie added his bit. "Tacking for the right approach."

Omoh at this point became uneasy, wondering whether that was just an innocent-sounding prelude to some more pointed observations. To his great relief, however, the conversation abruptly shifted focus. Big Jay had just recalled an incident which he had intended to recount some time ago, but had completely forgotten.

"Eh eh!" he interjected, his broad grin spreading slowly across his foliaged face, "I know a had something to tell you all."

Then after a brief pause, carefully calculated to arouse the interest of his listeners, he continued his tale, "The other night, as a cruising casually down First Avenue, guess who a spot coming the other direction?"

Then another of those calculated pauses occured fully achieving its desired effect. Big Jay seemed to be enjoying every minute of his performance.

"Remember the big redhead thing from up North? Ah-h-h! Yes, that one. Boy, she looking good fuh so. She walking up towards me on the driver's side, so a slow down and toot the horn—full of horniness meself."

Another pause. This time, a sharp raven-like crack of laughter broke the tension.

"You should 'ave seen how she jump! Ha. ha. And all the goodies shaking up like jelly. Ha ha ha. And then she look at the boy and would you believe . . . ."

Omoh listened intently as Big Jay, taking pains to make the necessary emphases, drew out the story. Fascinated, he watched the accompanying gesticulations that at times necessitated the use of both hands, resulting in the complete letting go of the steering wheel. But he was never worried, for the big Nash rolled on unerringly, quite confident in its knowledge of much-travelled ways.

After a while, Omoh's thoughts began to wander. Curly! He had quite forgotten her that day. How strange! Or was hers the face that smiled at him during his dream? Was hers the unheard voice that lured him on within his paradise? Were those her hands that raised him up so gently when all else seemed hopeless? Was it because of her—? But what was the use of pondering such things? He could never tell for sure.

Vaguely then he heard a cacophony of laughter and joined in the chorus quite instinctively. Big Jay, looking over his shoulder, coaxed the Nash into a space just barely long enough to accommodate it. Once the old car was safely parked, they emerged and stretched themselves. As they walked toward the restaurant, Big Jay looked back proudly at the parked car that would, for an hour or more, enjoy a rest it well deserved.

"Not bad at all, not bad at all," he congratulated himself, though actually somewhat surprised at his achievement.

"Not bad at all," the soft voice of Kopakie repeated parrot-like, "but once in a life time," it continued with a chuckle.

Still feigning self-confidence, Big Jay could only counter, "You know better than that, ole man."

Soon all three of them were seated in the reserve dining room, the more popular sections being all filled up. A meal for four was ordered so as to avoid the inconvenience of ordering extra portions afterwards.

"Aha, as a was saying just now."

Big Jay then calmly resumed the oral replay of his recent encounter with the big redhead, but only after a brief but careful recapitulation of all he had said before. Omoh listened for a while, but once again his thoughts returned to Curly.

Indeed, she seemed to like him. Why else had she consented to spend so special a day as Christmas with him? And moreover, she was sufficiently mature to know the facts of life. As far as he was concerned, the fact that she had once been married and had a teenage daughter was no problem whatsoever, though he was fully aware of what Ma Poppo and the others back home would say about that. Their interests were quite similar. She was creative—in fact, she painted beautifully. She loved music too and spoke of it with feeling and appreciation, whether it was jazz or classical. Besides, she played an instrument.

But then, such thinking was temporarily cut short. With renewed interest, Omoh listened to Big Jay's voice, then in full crescendo, approach the long-awaited climax. Fascinated once more, he watched his friend go through the final motions. And then, the atmosphere exploded with a sudden blast of laughter—laughter completely unrestrained. Down onto the table, black hands upon white linen tablecloth, and up and backwards to a most peculiar angle, the heads—all three of

Chinese Restaurant

them—moved in ritualistic manner, quite heedless of the many startled faces just turned in their direction and much paler than before.
Omoh and his two friends knew that many of those faces, despite their
apparent disapproval, would have liked to shed the mask of self-
control that they had worn since childhood and join in the happy
laughter.

Eventually, the laughter quite spent itself and silence, so rudely
ousted from the hallowed dining room just recently, immediately
returned. Reaching into his pocket, Big Jay pulled out a large and
brightly coloured handkerchief with which he wiped away the happy
tears that lingered on his darkly glistening cheeks. Kopakie, still shaking his head in disbelief, resumed his usual attitude of nonchalance.
Omoh, his head still resting on the table's edge next to the single fork
set out before him, began to wonder if perhaps they could have been a
little less uproarious. But soon. he raised himself up, thinking, "Oh,
what the hell! What's done is done, that's what. Who really cares a
damn?"

A few minutes later, the plates were set and the meal arrived. Palates
just sated with the taste of happy laughter cried out to have their fill of
that which disturbed them with its warm aroma. The waiter, for a
while, withheld the extra order, wondering if perchance he had made
some error. But Big Jay soon undid his fears.

"Just leave it there, old chap, in the empty space," he told the still-
puzzled youth. "We'll soon take care of it."

As the waiter, obviously a newcomer to the establishment, turned to
leave, he added, "Some hot sauce, if you please, Sir. The real hot stuff.
The hotter the better, Sir."

The young waiter, looking backwards at the group and wondering if
what he had heard was true, departed. Chuckling to themselves, the
boys dug into the assorted combination-meals that were piled high
upon the dishes. The waiter soon returned and, setting three separate
services of hot mustard upon the table, turned hurriedly to leave.
But Kopakie's voice, silken though raised in mild protest, delayed him,
"Hey Mr. Chin! Not mustard, miboy, but hot sauce!"

Then as the young man stared fixedly at him in total confusion, he
spoke again, "No wantee mustard. Askee boss-man for hot pepper
sauce—red hot pepper sauce, you hearee."

The rookie waiter, turning red himself and wondering perhaps what
turn of fate had brought that lot upon him, left once more in search of
the mysterious pepper sauce.

Not long afterwards, another more familiar face appeared and made
his way toward the table. In his hands, he carefully carried three small

55

shallow saucers of red liquid that looked like ordinary tomato paste but which, unlike tomato paste, could set a person's mouth on fire—unless that mouth had been already immunized by years of eating food quite liberally spiced with homemade red-hot pepper sauce.

"You satisfied now, you fellas?" inquired the familiar round face of the owner. "You give Ling hard time. Him new boy here, you know."

"Yup, everthing's okie dokie, now. We not know Ling is new boy here. Tell him we leave heap big tip for him. Okay?"

Big Jay, pausing just long enough to relay the sincere feelings of the threesome, immediately picked up the rhythm of his eating.

Bing, the boss, soon left, but only after he had admired for the umpteenth time the healthy appetites of his customers. Ling, once Bing had left, returned and, glancing cautiously at the group silently engaged in cutting down the mounds of food to nothing, turned and followed Bing into the kitchen.

Meanwhile, the plate in which the extra order had once proudly displayed itself looked embarassingly empty—a fitting tribute though to good food and hungry aliens in the big land.

* * *

The big blue Nash, true and faithful servant of four previous owners, relieved to have escaped the strain of climbing uphill, rolled smoothly down Tenth Avenue, its massive bulk gaining momentum with each turning of the wheels. The driver and present owner, comfortably reclined in post-prandial ease with long athletic legs stretched fully out beneath the panel, appeared somehow to be an innate feature of the aged mechanism. His casual attitude seemed to reflect the very nature of the car.

And so, Omoh and his two companions proceeded on to the second item on the evening's agenda—the casual visit to Sir Free. The familiar voice of Kopakie, humming an even more familiar tune, expressed the satisfaction not only of himself but of the entire unit—the car and complement. But unknown to Kopakie, that song became the prelude to the inevitable reappearance of Curly upon the stage of Omoh's consciousness.

There the well-formed figure glided about upon long slender legs, and Omoh (once again) applauded the simplicity of the outfit she so beautifully wore. The blonde hair—almost golden, though usually alive with frisky curls, was held in place by a ribbon around the head she carried tilted delicately to one side upon a long and slender neck. The smiling pixie face beamed with a youthful flush of colour that

56

veiled a known maturity, and Omoh (once again) admired the strict economy with which she had applied her makeup. The thick-nippled breasts, firmly imprinted on the silken blouse, performed a subtle minuet in rhythm with her movements.

With some uneasiness, Omoh watched as fascinated as before. And then he heard a voice—a voice not shrill with feminine excitability nor feeble with affected delicacy, but contralto-like. Its every word seemed to compose an aria in the opera of life. He heard it (as it had done some time ago) offer to spend the Christmas day with him:

"Omoh, now that your roommate's going to be away on Christmas day, why don't I come over to your place and make you a meal. My daughter has moved in with her dad's family for a while."

But (as before) he dared not trust his ears, lest they deceive him. And so, he muttered, softly to himself, "Wha—", then heard (once again) the offer made a second time. What luck! He had indeed turned down all previous invitations to share in yuletide celebrations. Besides, Kopakie had just recently accepted an invitation to dine with a close friend and his family that day.

Omoh then listened to another voice of the past that sounded strangely like his own (though somewhat shakier) inquire, "Do you really mean that, Curly?" And then, more:

"Why, surely I do, I would not have said that if I didn't."

"Well sure—yes sure, indeed. I'd love to have your company. Yes. You know, I could even invite a couple other friends over—guys who, like myself, were going to spend the day alone."

"Why, that's a good idea, Omoh . . . that's very thoughtful of you."

But then, he wondered (for the first time) if perhaps she really would have preferred to be with him alone. But alas! too late. He would never know.

Instead, right there before him as he sat in Big Jay's car, the entire Christmas day replayed itself. The darkly glowing faces of the half dozen young men (like himself far far away from home) who squeezed themselves into the basement apartment, the gaggle of excited voices vying with each other for priority of speech, the pleasant but unfamiliar smell of roast turkey mingled with other mouth-watering aromas, the rousing kick of strong drinks taken "on the rocks", the warmth of close companionship that dulled the ache of undeniable nostalgia, the calypsoes spontaneously made up in honour of the patron-hostess of the meal—all these and many others.

Squirming with reawakened gratitude, Omoh wished that he could one day find the courage to express to Curly the feelings he wanted to convey that day, but could not. And he determined that he would speak out the next time he saw her.

But then a sudden stop jolted him back into the living present. Big Jay, startled by the rashness of a bearded youth intent on beating a red light, had reacted with surprising quickness. His long leg, moving much faster then than it had ever done, had hit the brake quite firmly. The big Nash, unaccustomed to such unexpected calls to action, had responded promptly. But soon the big blue car resumed its journey at a pace much quicker than before. Indeed, it seemed quite anxious to escape the crowded roadways. The three young men, after-dinner drowsiness quite banished, came very much alive.

"But did you ever see me crosses! Just like that, this Mr. Man want to put me in trouble," Big Jay contemplated the close call.

"The bloody ass!" Omoh exclaimed, "Suppose the brakes didn't hold."

"You know I could 'ave killed the man," mused Big Jay.

"I bet he hasn't got some special deadline," Kopakie offered, "except perhaps an appointment with the old man upstairs."

"Boy, I didn't know the old Nash was in such good shape. She stopped on the dot," observer Omoh.

"What! you kidding or what!" queried Big Jay. "The ole gal got new parts all over."

"Better than the owner," added Kopakie. "You know, Omoh, it's Big Jay who surprised me—not the car. Don't think I ever seen him move so fast."

"Not even on the track!" asked Omoh with a wink.

"Especially on the track—that's what I mean," Kopakie explained.

"Jealousy, that's all. And jealousy will get you nowhere, fellas."

Despite the near-tragic interlude, however, Omoh could not black out the vivid recall of his first meeting with Curly. It was Saturday evening, some hours after he had written the last of his Christmas examinations, at an impromptu party he had gone to with Kopakie and Big Jay.

When they arrived, the party had been going on for some time. On entering, Omoh could not distinguish any faces in the swirl of people dancing in a yellow mist. He felt his eyes begin to smart from the acrid fumes that hung stagnant in the dimly lit room. Small intermittent glows of light, like fireflies in country fields at night, betrayed the guilty smokers.

Cuddling a drink in his hands, Omoh watched his companions go off to greet old friends he did not know. He let himself flop wearily down into a large armchair, which at various spots revealed the stuffings of its bloated interior. A hand-me-down, for certain, Omoh surmised. Must have previously belonged to older and more wealthy relatives of the gal who now owned it.

But there! Not far away and extended toward him! A pair of legs—long shapely legs! Omoh allowed his eyes (now accustomed to the dimness) to travel swiftly up along the rest of the anatomy. But within seconds, they came to an embarrassed halt, arrested by the full bosom that blossomed into view.

"My God!" he silently exclaimed, turning his eyes abruptly elsewhere, "what pins! what comforters!"

Already he could feel his parts begin to rise up in honour of such new-found beauty. Disturbed, he struggled to control himself, but found that long suffering had made it difficult. What if the proud owner had seen him enter and sit down, then observed his every action so far? Despite his fears, he had to see the face that made the figure whole. He would just have to risk the possibility of confrontation face-to-face.

Anxiety quite ruffled him and, for a while, he kept his gaze elsewhere. Then casually, as if in search of a familiar face, he turned his head around in the direction of the so-far-headless form. But much to his dismay, no legs, no juicy busts, nor angel face came into sight! The empty chair before him looked most grotesque—completely out of place.

Intensely disappointed, Omoh slumped deep down into the large armchair that had seen better times. Staring down at the floor, he sought comfort in the drink he had not tasted yet. But there, incredibly! those shapely legs again—this time, however, moving briskly to a routine of dance. This time, Omoh resolved, he would not let his shyness rob him of a pleasure he knew would be a rare one.

And soon, indeed, he looked up boldly and, for the first time, saw the smiling pixie face. Beneath a blond, almost golden, head of frisky curls, it calmy contemplated a rather uneven head that snuggled up against the bosom beneath it. Watching, Omoh felt a thump, a flutter and a sudden whang! How could that horrendous head so trespass upon sacred place! How could it dare to defile such ideal presences!

* * *

Sitting there in the back seat of the Nash that fast approached its target torpedo-like, Omoh vividly recalled the strong urge he felt that night to smash the head and perhaps take its place. But he remembered too the inexplicable fears that had restrained him later on from going up to her and asking for a dance.

In fact, he had resigned himself to sitting there in the armchair and secretly admiring the long shapely legs, the eyes alive with warmth and love of life, the pixie smile that never seemed to fade, the almost golden curls that frisked about so restlessly, the slender neck of Grecian mould, the head held high and to one side, the full-nippled breast—the almost perfect figure not far away from him, yet so far beyond his reach.

And so he watched her easy-flowing motion, feeling all the while that somehow she never was at ease with any of her partners. But one time as she gracefully whirled past him, he saw (or rather, thought he saw) her look at him with curious, almost ogling eyes. Another time, he saw (or rather, thought he saw) her nod her head ever so slightly at him in apparent acknowledgment of his constant admiration.

But no, this could not be. She had never seen him anywhere before. Besides, how could he ever be worthy of such a special compliment? Even if what he saw (or rather, what he thought he saw) was true, was she not just being friendly to all the boys alike? Indeed, he had just overheard someone saying that she was and had been for a long time the hostess' best friend.

But another smile just then! This time, no doubt about it. It was meant for him! But was it just a casual smile of friendly welcome or a more deliberate gesture of interest or possible affection? Alas! he could not tell. But neither did he care. That smile! It could be meant for no one else, for there was no one else nearby just then. Yet he must take care not to make a complete ass of himself. He must be cautious.

The music played on and on. Curly, clutched in a firm embrace by another suitor, danced effortlessly on and on. Then as she passed close by another time, she deliberately turned her partner round about and looked unmistakably in Omoh's direction. Touched by the cordiality that flickered from her eyes, he dared to move his lips in silent asking for a dance.

Imagine his misgivings when a look of mild bewilderment replaced the smile upon her face! He could not repeat the question. What if the words just breathed along their silent path had found their mark, but there had stirred some mild rebuff? He could never risk a second slighting from someone so rare.

Besides, her partner, instinctively alerted to the threat of competition, had turned her the other way and fixed his eyes with obvious disapproval upon the puzzled Omoh. Like some young urchin caught at something he knew to be forbidden, Omoh could not disguise his guilt. Shifting with embarrassment, he watched his jealous rival steer the pixie-smiling Curly (much too roughly!) through a maze of dancers to the far side of the room.

For the next few seconds, Omoh could not avert his eyes from where he had seen her before she disappeared. But then Sir Free, who had spent the earlier hours of the party sipping drinks, old-talking and watching carefully for interesting developments, approached Omoh and sat beside him. Omoh, though happy to have someone to talk with, could not forget Sir Free's well-established reputation. He could not forget his gift of accurate perception nor his sharp-witted tongue. But most of all, he could not forget that right forefinger, crooked at the first joint, with which he had transfixed so many squirming victims.

Now more than ever, Omoh realized, he must conceal his feelings. He hoped, moreover, that Sir Free had not observed his recent behaviour. And he felt much better once he received the customary greeting, "So, what's happening, Omes miboy!"

Sir Free seemed to be in quite a party mood. His talk, accompanied by the usual histrionics, flowed more easily than usual. Taking hold of Omoh's shoulders, he drew him up and closer to him, then whispered in his ear, "Say, 'Mo, how d'you like that stuff across the way? The one with Lumpy. That is woman, eh!"

Guided by the notorious finger and the flashing eyes, Omoh looked eagerly among the dancers that swayed and bumped against each other. And (much to his surprise!) he saw the lovely Curly. But he also recognized her partner as the very person who had steered her off, away from his adoring glances.

Omoh allowed his eyes, once they survived the shock, to take their fill of her, and he would have done so longer had not a soft chuckle nearby interrupted him. Feigning nonchalance, he turned to face Sir Free. A quivering sent a chill up and down his spine. There before him, not ten inches away! a finger levelled at his nose and crooked at the first joint.

Omoh felt lost, thinking, "Not now," almost aloud.

* * *

"So, you've got it too," the chuckling observed. "Don't worry, lad, you ain't the only cat that's got it bad. Even the great one has the bug— and that ain't good."

Omoh could find no words of reply, so relieved was he—and grateful. To whom? He did not know. But just imagine, Sir Free admitting such a thing about himself. Omoh could hardly believe it. The fatal finger, though not generally fickle, had withdrawn itself quite unexpectedly. Meanwhile, Sir Free moved closer to Omoh and, in a lowered tone of voice, revealed to him the details he so longed to hear.

He told how Lengths, who had some time ago received his Bachelor's degree and was teaching somewhere in the province, had first brought her to a party last year. How all the boys had gone crazy over her that night and ever since, how she had absolutely but most pleasantly discouraged all advances out of loyalty to Lengths, how all details of her marriage and subsequent divorce had come to light eventually—though no one loved her less because of that, how Length's weekend visits to the city had recently become increasingly irregular, how as a result of that her many wooers had stepped up their wily campaigns to win her, how also . . . .

Sir Free's voice faded into silence. Omoh could feel his hold upon his shoulder tighten significantly. And then his voice, still lowered but urgent and surprised, exclaimed,

"But 'Mo, you are a hell of a sly one, man!"

Completely bewildered, Omoh could only blurt out, "What! Me? Wha' d' you mean? What have I done now?"

Shaking his head slowly from left to right and smiling mischievously, Sir Free continued, "Here I am, like some cunu-munu giving you the lowdown on the woman and all the time trying to catch her eyes, and just when I finally succeed she motioning to you. Ha ha. Well, I never see dat! Dat's one on the ole man—on de greatest!"

A warm rush of blood flooded Omoh's cheeks but, finding no pallidness to flush, it set them afire. The music stopped and the couples who had just enjoyed the last of a series of long-playing records ambled to their seats or made their way into the kitchen-turned-bar.

Sir Free rose to his feet and raised the still-befuddled Omoh by the shoulder he still held. And there before them stood the lovely Curly—even more beautiful than before! Omoh could not bring himself to look here in the eye—the very woman he had so ardently admired from the distance. A sudden acceleration of his blood intensified his heartbeat and quite upset the rhythm of his pulse. Its heavy beat, reaching quite deep within him, shook him up. He could hardly hold himself upright.

"So how are you, Sir Free?" he heard the firm but calm contralto inquire.

"Not nearly as well and blooming as you are, m'lady. But all the better now for seeing you," Sir Free replied with all the polish of a suave old pro.

"Still the greater flatterer, I see. Always was and always will be," the dialogue continued.

"Not falttery, my dear, but just the humble words of one who appreciates true beauty. Pity 'tis that I am not a poet to speak of you in verse."

Omoh listened quietly, fascinated by the sudden change of speech on Sir Free's part.

"Ha ha ha," the contralto rang out in all its richness. "Sir Free, you are a riot. I wonder what the girls would do without you around to boost their egos every now and then."

And before Sir Free could further eulogize the glories of womanhood. the contralto continued, "Who is your quiet friend, Sir Free? He seems to be quite shy—so much unlike you. I haven't seen him around before."

By then Omoh had composed himself as much as possible. In fact, he had thoroughly enjoyed the recent repartee. But, on hearing Curly ask about him, he began to waver.

Sir Free, though somewhat put off by the sudden termination of the kind of dialogue he revelled in, soon adjusted to the new role demanded of him. Placing his hands upon his heart and grimacing as though it pained him terribly, he exclaimed, "How can I ever compensate, madame, for such an oversight. You see, that's what your mere presence does to me."

Then with great formality, he performed the ritual of introduction, "Curly, this is Omoh, another jewel come to the big land from the Rock. A scholar and a gentleman besides his other talents. Omoh of recent arrival from the Rock, meet Curly, lovely native of the big land—the loveliest of all her sex, I do believe."

Before Omoh could say his part, Curly, extending her long arms, remarked, "Glad to know you, Omoh." Then with a twinkle in her eyes that sparkled from the pixie-smiling face, she added, "And I would like to dance with you—that is, of course, if you still would like me to do so. I think I read your lips correctly."

As she turned to lead the way onto the dance floor, Omoh saw Sir Free standing there, the famed forefinger slow scratching his fast-balding head and heard him whisper in a more familiar parlance.

"Mo, Mo, you son of a b., you must be born with a gold spoon in yuh mouth."

Omoh himself, meanwhile, shaking with a surge of passion which her warm hands aroused in him, could just barely mumble, "Thank you very much. I am indeed most happy to have met you, and I would dearly love to dance with you."

A chuckle close by called attention to the fact that Sir Free had gathered new weapons for his arsenal. But Omoh did not care one jot. The self-appointed disc-jockey for the night, a chubby round-faced Chinese youth, had got his next selection of long-playing records going.

Gathering himself together, Omoh moved closely behind Curly to the already crowded floor. Then with new-found confidence, he took his pixie-smiling partner into his arms for his first (but by no means last) dance of the night.

Sir Free, still taken aback by the recent turn of events, stood looking curiously at them. One of his hands was pushed deep down into his pocket, the other kept the glass in which his drink had already been diluted by melting ice. Glancing then at him, Omoh (for the first time) observed an obvious curvature of legs and (for the first time too) the odd way in which his shoe-tips pointed inwards, as if in silent admiration of each other.

And so it was that Omoh danced with curly that night on which they first met. To those of his rivals who could surmount their petty jealousies, he assumed a new identity as someone to be respected and admired. To the others who could not, he became a person to be watched and avoided at future parties.

That was the night that they told each other of their separate pasts, of their many hopes and fears, of their various likes and dislikes. That was the night on which they both expressed their need for someone much closer—she confessing that she could not maintain her loyalty much longer to someone she so rarely saw, and he admitting how difficult it was to keep on being faithful to people far away he could not see, much less touch. And that night he banished from his mind the admonitions that he knew Ma Poppo would repeat if she were close by—Ma Poppo whom he had not kissed that day of his departure. That night too, he banished from his mind the haunting memory of Janice and Mildred, neither of whom he had bothered to kiss that day of his departure.

* * *

Such things Omoh had experienced some time ago back in the big land. I could go on to tell you everything about his past and present too, and Omoh would not mind it. But my intent is not to fabricate an exact replica of the man. Instead, I hope, through a careful selection of details, to make you understand more clearly why he sits there still slumped over on his desk and why I still would like to pick him up and take him to his bed that he may rest more comfortably.

At times during the first year of his visit to the big land, the jigsaw of his life fell into place quite unexpectedly. That night he first saw Curly was such a time. At other times, however, the dice all rolled awry, the cards dropped out of the desired sequence and the pins, though firmly struck, remained upright.

Later, as the snowball of his life within the big land rolled along in its rapidly expanding bulk, the pieces of life's puzzle seemed to fit more rarely. And even when they did, the picture they formed was far from

64

comforting. Even as I tell you this, an image flashes by before me. I see him walking on the campus grounds, listening as his thoughts resound within the chambers of his consciousness.

The day before, the day before that too (in fact, for many days before), the rain had kept on falling on the land that had been toughened somewhat by the winter's chill of previous days. So lightly had it fallen that it seemed to have escaped detection by the inmates of the many buildings—those busy ones who watched each day the reruns of each other's life.

Not so the rain in other distant lands, when suddenly the sun that usually displays itself high up against a brilliant sky blue withdraws itself and sulks behind dark mounds of cloud, from which large drops like giant tears soon fall with stinging vengeance down upon the guilty world beneath. Stunned silence then prevails within the crowded homes, as roofs of 'galvanize' ring out in loud protests against the sudden downpour. The narrow streets, miraculously emptied of the crowds of cyclists and pedestrians, of loafers and street-vendors, enjoy the cleansing waters that querulously rush along their lengths in fast-increasing volumes. Few children here and there expose their naked bodies to the drenching, cavorting gaily up and down back yards or busily engage in make-believe boat racing down the narrow gutters. In every doorway, bright shining faces touched by nature's exuberance can be observed. There a youngster neatly clad and on his way to school. On one side of him, a chubby civil servant on her way to selling stamps and, on the other side, a small-town executive preoccupied with keeping clean his patent leather shoes. No one worries then, for they know that the customary pace of life (steady but not hysterical) would be suspended until the showers ceased not long now. And true enough, within half an hour, the sun—no longer sullen—peers through the breaking clouds and, not seeing the eager faces nor the loosely swaggering bodies he so dearly loves, he quickly burns the rain away and dries the moisture from the land that glistens greener then.

Omoh noticed, as he walked that day that the land had already thawed itself out—not because of any great intensity of heat but because it had not quite frozen up during the winter—if one could lend such appellation to a season not even long enough to necessitate the purchasing of heavy coats. In fact, being thirsty, the land had swallowed up the many puddles of the previous days.

Around the campus, the day displayed all its vernal finery. The brightly coloured flowers, arranged (somewhat prematurely) in various patterns, paid tribute to the gardeners and landscapers around; bird-songs, not readily identifiable by the immigrants from tropic lands, kept up a welcome counterpoint to the monotone of water tricklig from a nearby stream into a lily pond (the freshman's Waterloo); and the campus folk, students and faculty alike, touched by the vibrancy that stirred all things that day, had shed their wintry dullness and flitted spryly about in lighter, brighter outfits. Scattered on the grass that had been wet with rain just recently in couples and in larger groups (and alone in rare instances), pale bodies greedily absorbed the sunlight, seeking a duskiness they despised in others. Strange world, thought Omoh, when others blessed with swarthiness often wished to blanch themselves. *football*

On a field nearby, the more athletic types were busily engaged in hurling catching dropping cuddling and running with a strangely elongated ball. Ocassionally, a couple, hand in hand, ambled along in silent contact. And over there, five men lifted chunks of rolled ruglike turf from a truck and fitted them expertly into patches cut neatly in the spacious lawn. Amazing! *grass*

Along the beach, not far away, many more enjoyed the day's serenity, sitting in parked cars or running on the shore or straddling logs that had escaped some broken boom and come safely to land. But no one dared to swim. They wisely shunned the tranquil and inviting water that had been flooded by the recent thawing further north.

For a long while that day, Omoh walked on and listened to his many thoughts. Across the shimmering water, he saw the thriving city outlined, the sounds of its busy life quite muted by the distance. Stopping for a moment, he turned full circle, nodded his head and then continued walking.

On such days as this, his thoughts continued, (and in such places too) one could go on walking on and on without thinking that one is walking and not even asking why one lets oneself go walking on and on nor wondering what else one could or should be doing not stopping to observe this item here that there or to take note of this person (or that creature) doing (or not doing) this (or that) but just walking on and on and seeing all there is around and smelling all the odours and hearing all the sounds and tasting and feeling everything (or nothing) without trying to distinguish this from that or to compare this object with another there or questioning this presence here (or absence there) not trying to recall the night that was nor yesterday nor any previous time not thinking of the night to come nor of tomorrow nor of the future further off. For then who I am and where I am and whither I am going and whence I have come all would be of no importance (not even am I still walking or not) for I would be an indistinguishable part of all—all persons and all objects—a part of present past and future (and of space) and so I and am and was and will be all would be irrevocably bound together. But walking is just I in action an walking leads from here to there from somewhere now to elsewhere then and stopping sometimes must take place (often without asking why) and starting once again and stopping and starting on and on until one day stopping becomes permanent and starting discontinues. And so since walking is but I in action and stopping will one day occur who I am and wherefore are important— so too what time it is and where I am and whence I came and whither I am going. Yet one must understand and keep in mind that one is part of all that is and so though thinking must take place (and questioning) one must be sure to hear and see to feel and smell and taste and so to be aware of everything and everyone and of oneself within them all. And perhaps then and only then one may begin to know what I am means and why too there is walking (and stopping too) which like thinking leads to detours and dead-ends and finally to full stops—

Omoh kept walking on and on that day, for a long while thinking nothing but observing and enjoying everything around. But thinking eventually intruded once again upon the tranquil mind, asking many questions and demanding answers.

"Who am I, indeed?"

"Just a foreign student," he heard the startled self reply.

"Whence came I?"

"From the Rock far far away."

"Where am I now?"

"Here in the big land among millions of strange faces."

"Whither am I headed?"

"Hopefully towards graduation in medical studies and then to return home as a doctor."

"What time is it?"

"Just some day in early spring not even midway in my pre-med training."

Then thinking temporarily ceased its cross-examination, as Omoh stopped and inhaled deeply, hoping thereby to cut short such agonizing probing of the self. But thinking recommenced, reminding him that to reach one's destination one has to stop at times to do such necessary things as reading writing learning studying and so on.

"But wherefore?" he heard the question asked. "How do such things affect I am in terms of all and was and will be?"

To this stern reason countered, "Surely now, by finding out and practising the art of curing ailments, of mending broken bones and correcting the malfunctioning of vital organs, one enables others to find the strength to go on walking on and on."

"But what of feeling and of being quite aware of what such walking means? How can one help others in such things by stopping to hear lectures, to read books, to answer questions on material taught by others often much less sensitive and to eventually discover how to patch up and mend and even to make whole again impaired flesh and bones?"

Thinking then faltered once again and questioning desisted, as Omoh sought refuge in being part of all, no longer preoccupied with the awareness of I am but completely absorbed into the harmony of being.

* * *

Registration the second time around turned out to be just as frustrating and tedious as the first time. Standing in the long lines that snaked their way around and in between the make-shift counters set up within the large dark armory (long emptied of its stock but no less sinister) Omoh recalled the disillusionment he had suffered that very day a year ago. He wondered whether the unfolding of time had altered anything.

The rain was falling as it did that other day, the faces of students and administrators alike seemed to be equally forlorn and bored with the proceedings, their bodies moved no less like automatons. In truth and fact, the entire—

What then had changed? For one thing, he himself had resolved upon a change of faculty, despite expostulations on the part of friends, instructors and others who were acquainted with his first year successes. What else? What, if anything, had he achieved? Had it been really worth the while to have moved so far away from home and all the loved ones (whom he had not written to for quite some time), so far away from all the many happenings (unpressured but eventful) that had been his previous life.

Jostled roughly from behind, Omoh found himself pushed tightly up against one of the makeshift counters. Accepting a multi-coloured booklet, he began to write and then rewrite and write again the information requested by the many administrative departments: Name . . . Date of Birth . . .

"My God!" a sudden recognition phrased itself, "I'm getting old as hell—and damn fast too!"

Omoh had always realized that he exceeded the average age of students at his level. That, however, did not bother him. He never once regretted the many and widely varied activities that he had pursued after leaving college (or high school as the natives of the big land call it). In fact, he had learned enough of life to compensate for the late

68

commencement of his university career. So often had he noticed how the younger ones straight from high school were handicapped by their inexperience. Besides, he had to earn enough to cover all first year expenses before he could receive permission to come abroad.

Shrugging his shoulders as he was wont to do at times of meditation, Omoh recalled the more recent past—those few months of summer spent among the lesser mortals such as stevedores, construction men and hyped-up small-time musicians. Indeed, he had learned as much (or more perhaps) from his experiences those days as he had done during his earlier activities within the intellectual scene.

Soon, he answered the last question and closed the multi-coloured booklet. Instantly, as if a sleeping monster had come to life quite suddenly, the long line of human bodies shuffled on a pace or two, squeezing him out, then ceased its effort once again.

Moving forward slowly, Omoh surveyed the vastness of the old square building that kept out the lightly falling rain but not the insidious chill. And soon he heard the sound of marching shouting marching stopping marching turning stopping standing easy snapping to attention and marching on again! Startled, he no longer beheld long lines of students bleary-eyed and dishevelled with fatigue, but men in uniforms with their youthful faces flushed beneath their neatly cropped blonde hair—eager aspirants to military glory, conjured up by the nature of the place. But before his swiftly blinking eyes could hold themselves full open, the marching stopped and the strange forms disappeared just as unexpectedly as they had recently appeared.

In their stead, pale ghostly faces all around stared vacantly from bleary eyes, the monotone of shuffling feet and tired voices filled up the room again and, in the close and stifling air, strong scents of expensive perfumes and lotions and of cheaper deodorants and hair sprays strove unsuccessfully to neutralize the more natural smells of human ear lobes, armpits, crotches, mouths and asses.

Arriving at the empty space before the nearest exit, Omoh sighed with great relief. Like a late-emerging chrysalis, he hurried through the doorway, seeking fresher air. Instead, much to his surprise (for he had quite forgotten this aspect of the yearly ritual), he found himself confronted by a raincoated mob. A motley group of students, like amateur salesmen all hustling shouting grabbing pushing, tried desperately to win subscribers to the various student publications and purchasers for the many season tickets to the various on-campus events scheduled for the coming year. Omoh, however, like the others who had just escaped the ordeal within the building, was in no mood for bargaining—especially since he had so little money left after paying the term's fees.

Wrapping his thin coat closely round his body, Omoh put his head down and began to butt his way through the rain-soaked bodies. After some small success, he felt his progress rudely halted, as some overly enthusiastic youngster, determined to excel in rushing for fraternity recruits, grabbed him from behind. Omoh turned angrily to confront the apparent assailant, but looked directly into a pair of blue eyes dilated with surprise and white with fear.

"Exc-c-cuse me, Sir," the stammerer apologized, "You see, I thought you were somebody else."

"Who did you think I was?"

Omoh no longer felt exasperated by what he had mistaken for an unprovoked attack. He had sized up the situation and made up his mind to play a part.

"N-no one in p-p-particular, Sir!" the stammerer continued weakly. "I just thought you you were wh—"

"I was who?" Omoh fired back, allowing the young man no opportunity of recovering from his near-fatal mistake.

"I just thought that you were one of us," the lad explained, no longer stammering but pointing to the pin he wore (so proudly a while ago) and releasing the hold he had unconsciously maintained on Omoh's coat.

"One of whom?" Omoh persisted.

Recognizing then the trap which he himself had sprung, the young enthusiast turned suddenly to run away. But Omoh, reacting much more swiftly, had grasped his wrists with both his bony, claw-like hands.

"Aren't you going to invite me to become your brother, brother?" he asked in a much softer tone of voice.

Omoh could not tell whether the water on the victim's face was rain or perspiration (despite the chilly weather). But thinking that he had played his part successfully enough, he felt a genuine sorrow for the lad. Slackening his grip on his wrist somewhat, he winked at him and spoke as if in consolation.

"It's okay, man. No problems. I don't really want to wear your pin, today or evermore. It's not my kind of thing, you see."

Watching the tense face slowly relax itself into a rather innocent and handsome smile, he added, "No hard feelings, man. I understand your problem, and I really do feel sorry for you. So relax and think about it, man."

Accepting the hand that he had just released but which the blushing face had extended to him, Omoh shook it firmly, then turned and made his way on through the crowd, his head still bent forward as if to butt.

In a few moments he passed between the neighbouring buildings and wove his way between the cars jammed tightly in the parking lot. Eventually, he stopped and raised his head, smiling at the recent interlude. But soon the happiness achieved at the expense of one so innocent began to cloy.

After brief consultation with himself, Omoh headed for the nearest bus stop, intent on going home. For, during that period of his life, whenever circumstances proved to be discomforting in any way, he always withdrew (almost instinctively) down into the basement room off-campus that he called home—a room still dimly lit and dingy-looking but warm and comfortable with lingering smells of highly seasoned food.

Once there, he knew, he could enjoy his little world of privacy and solitude or he could choose to journey far off into worlds of past, of present and of future that thrived within the pages of the books he dearly loved. In such worlds, he then believed, one could allow oneself to grow enraptured without fear of being made too uncomfortably aware of one's own troubled self. At times, he knew full well, one could encounter aspects of oneself developed (for better or for worse) in some character. At other times, one could detect some quality one always longed to have but was denied or else another trait which one quite fortunately never did possess—or, having once possessed, had long since relinquished.

* * *

Riding on the yellow bus that bumped its unhurried way toward the campus gates, where he would make connections with the city buses that would travel at a livelier pace downhill, Omoh stared blankly at the falling rain. He heard the rumble of the engine all but drown out the soft staccato of its fall against the metal sides. And for a while he felt himself being lulled to sleep.

But soon the peaceful overture was interrupted by recollections that forced themselves in bustling throngs upon his vacant mind. Faces smiling and unsmiling, bodies of different shapes and sizes, places pleasant and unpleasant, and situations—some more comforting and others hopelessly involved.

Never before that summer had Omoh suffered the anxiety of wondering whether he could pay his next month's rent! Never before his advent to the big land had he been forced to wonder whether there would be a meal for him on any given day! Nor had he actually believed that such things could ever happen to him.

Yet for such disillusionment there was some recompense, for he had learned to modify the tenor of his life. He had discovered how to sacrifice the excesses of the three-meals-a-day routine he had practised all his life, how to regard each meal (in fact, each morsel of each meal) as precious, how to be less picky in his choice of foods, and how to forego the luxury of alcoholic drinks he could not really afford. What's more, he had perceived again (and even more clearly than before) the true essence of good friendship—friendship oftentimes engendered by the emergencies of daily intercourse.

Omoh recalled, without regret or bitterness, the many long hours he had spent providing entertainment for the largely teenaged audiences in order to receive a small percentage of the gate receipts. Often a three-night weekend stint did not even provide what would be considered minimum wages for an ordinary day's work. The youthful bodies, tinged with the greenish red of coloured lights, swayed awkwardly in silent contemplation of glasses of soft drinks that stood upon the barrel tops beside them. He heard them clapping (often with disastrous results) to the rhythms he banged out upon the untuned piano, and listened to the steady thump thumping of the native island drum which Big Jay coddled lovingly between his long athletic legs.

Omoh felt, indeed, that it had been reward enough just to have entertained so many (or so few) regardless of their ages, to have had the privilege of letting them see and hear and feel and be aware of all that he was then (and always had been and would continue to be), to have moved each and every one around to feel that they were living then and not merely existing, and thereby to have rescued them (though temporarily) from the tedium of routine and the strictures of convention. For then and only then did their real selves (what they always had been and would continue to be) rise up and manifest themselves completely.

As he walked the short distance from the bus stop to his home, Omoh could not distinctly remember when he had changed buses, travelled downhill and eventually dismounted. Nor did it really matter to him. What mattered was that he still walked. For he had also (once again) indulged himself in remembrances of two close brushes he had had with death that summer. And (once again) his eyes bedewed themselves with gratitude—to whom he knew not. For walking, on each of those occasions, could easily have ceased.

Remembering, Omoh walked on with greater urgency, feeling a stronger passion for all creatures and all things around him. He quite forgot the boredom and the anger, the frustration and the disillusionment of registration days. The very wetness of the day no longer felt discomforting. Instead, he welcomed it, acknowledging the promise of fulfillment that always came with rain and thinking how fortunate he was to still be walking.

But not long after, what he had been that summer (and how and where) revealed itself (for yet another time) before his eyes, while he attended and endured again the full range of emotions that he had experienced on those two particular occasions. For some time, he was not even conscious of what the present was (not even of the lightly drizzling rain nor the wetness of his clothes) as he watched himself there within the hollow of a ship, sitting on a temporary platform built up with flour bags and watching with admiration the members of the other gang across the way lifting the heavy bags and piling them high, one on the other and—

and himself not hearing (or rather, hearing but not making out) the winchman's cry of "Headsup!" a warning well-known by all dockworkers (except perhaps the newly hired hands as he was) and failing to recognize the meaning of the seemingly wild antics of the others nearby until some providence or seventh sense or perhaps chance turned his head around in time to see a thick wooden tray, heavy with its complement of bags, come whizzing down the hatchway close to his left ear and across to the far side of the hole where, ceasing its rapid motion, it was seized by strong hands and guided safely to another platform like the one on which he sat benumbed with shock and—

and slowly realizing the great danger that he had just been in and hearing too the angry voices of the older more experienced men and feeling miserable and stupid yet understanding soon that those sharp words were being hurled not at him but at the winchman up above who (as they argued) should have somehow recognized the presence of first-timers and should have exercised much greater caution in sending down the loads and—

and then feeling somewhat guilty not knowing what to say or do but seeing everything return to normalcy quite soon and joining in and realizing then that the entire nightmare which seemed so long-protracted had only lasted several minutes.

Remembering all and enduring the strong emotions he had felt that day, Omoh walked on, but soon awakened to the reality of his present being. He felt a most uncomfortable dampness that was not the wetness of his rain-soaked clothes but instead a clamminess that he had sweated recently. Looking round about he saw that he was just a little more than half way home. But he had not progressed much further before the second portion of the double feature began its inevitable replay.

And so once again, within a few minutes, Omoh looked on as what he had been that summer reproduced itself. He watched himself in apparent miniature poised carefully upon the topmost rung of the narrow ladder that reached deep into the ship's hole, hearing the ship itself groan constantly as if it pained to have such probing of its gaping womb, but feeling all the while its gentle rhythmic sway and roll and understanding too why ships were seen as female and—

and still watching his small self begin the slow descent much deeper than ever before and trying to act normally but feeling trepidation, such as he had felt that day long ago when with a boy-scout's daring he had mounted up some wartime structure that reared its shrinking bulk high upon a hillock overlooking a small village near the sea far down below but had completely frozen-up on looking down as the wind tugged violently at his frail youthful self and—

and then observing his even smaller self arriving safely at the bottom of the ship and looking way up at the clear patch of sky above and wondering just how far down under water he had come, but soon working with the others lifting bags of flour (once again) and carrying them in under the hatches and placing them neatly upon the very bottom of the ship and observing all the while how slowly but surely the level of the bags rose upwards and—

and seeing then his tiny self sit down eventually in sheer exhaustion upon the bags beneath the hatch where only a small triangle of light from above could be perceived and hearing someone of European stock protest as best he could in broken English freely spiced with loud obscenities the loss of bets that he had placed the day before and laughing as he demonstrated how "de big bum" on whom his money rode had fallen heavily on "hees fat awse" and lain there with twitching feet for the count of ten but—

but hearing then a more familiar voice suggesting that perhaps they had not chosen a safe place to rest on after all and smiling in mild contempt of Big Jay's unwarranted anxiety but yielding to his friend's insistence that they move further inwards under the protective beams intending though to tease him later on for being so grandmother-like then

then staring calmly at the loaded tray that had come into view and wondering what unsteady or pendulumlike and—careless hands permitted it to swing so freely

and watching completely mesmerized the white dust that spiralled upwards and mushroomed like mini-Hiroshima-atom-bomb up from the very spot where he just recently sat and seeing also though a haze an object rolling clumsily in helter-skelter cartwheels crushing bursting everything before it then bumping with a sickening thud against the ship's side and falling finally inert upon a heap of broken bags and—

and recognizing Big Jay's face gone strangely pale, staring preoc-

74

cupied with obvious thoughts and questionings at the very spot where they once sat, then sunken deep and covered with flour spurted from the broken bags but—

but seeing them on that very spot a small pool of gore made thicker with the white matter that had spilled from the empty grinning skull hanging loosely from the broken body nearby that looked so much like him and feeling too his stomach heave itself upwards twice in vain efforts to spew out the sickness that it felt.

As if what he saw and felt were no longer phantoms of a reality that had been but had ceased to be, Omoh tasted the fresh oozings of saliva go sour in his mouth and felt the queasy undulations of his stomach threaten to embarass him. How fortunate, he thought as he walked along, that he had not yet eaten anything that day. But suddenly, with a muffled cry, he stayed the lifted foot that would have moved him forward and held his eyes in steady focus there upon a spot in front of him where he saw (or thought he saw) a shattered skull that hung twisted at an awkward angle from a limp body that seemed much like his own.

Staring at the twin image of himself, Omoh stood motionless, unable to complete the step he had begun. Thinking had ceased as well, as vivid recollection seemed to have arrested all present consciousness and functioning of self. But only for a brief while, indeed! for the intensity of such recall soon burned itself out and walking recommenced, almost as if it had never been suspended. Omoh felt a strange sensation run through his entire body. Quickly he looked about him to see if by some chance someone had witnessed his apparently unnatural conduct. Fortunately, no one had done so.

Omoh was actually quite tired—not so much physically as emotionally, as if he had just undergone several hours without interruption of third degree interrogation under the full glare of brightly burning lights. Not long after, however, he turned into the narrow entrance to his apartment, pushed the side door open and tumbled down the stairway on into the make-shift toilet. Shut within the acrid darkness, he sat thinking nothing and doing nothing, except staring at the little light that forced itself in through one of the many cracks.

Some time afterwards he got up, pulled on his pants and walked through the empty basement into the precincts of his room, feeling somehow relieved. Without switching on the light or taking off his dampened clothes, he let himself slump heavily onto the creaking couch and lie motionless. But soon the very walls (though dingy and ugly with peeling paint), the linoleum on the floor (though broken and uneven with the several previous layers peeping through at every crack), the grimy gas range (though dangerous with its broken controls

75

and bare flame), the very air itself (though close and heavy with the smell of recent frying)—all these familiar things gave comfort to his trembling form and made him feel secure.

And so, Omoh straightened himself out and stretched his limbs full upwards, standing high on tiptoes. He switched on the lights and changed his clothes, hanging the damp garments on the line that stretched diagonally across the empty section of the basement.

Soon he began to whistle—not any well-known melody that he had heard before, but fitful flights of notes. Smiling, he tried to conjure up his first day on the docks, remembering how rudely he had been awakened that morning from a sleep he had begun only two hours before, how excited he had been on learning that new hands were being taken on, how apprehensively he had watched the grains of wheat come shooting down the chute and forming a cone-shaped mound like a giant ant-hill that he would have to level off, how anxiously he had wondered if the man at the controls would be sufficiently alert to halt the whispering onrush before it buried him and the other members of the gang alive within the narrow hole, how tickled he had been (though quite exhausted) later in the afternoon to see his friends covered from head to foot with white dust, forgetting meanwhile that he himself looked just as funny.

Omoh also remembered how quickly and earnestly the workers had performed their tasks, even in the absence of the foremen. So very much unlike their counterparts back home where tropic temperatures and different attitudes to life necessitated a more relaxed and inter-mittent pace of work. Reaching into his wallet, he removed the card which identified him as a member of the shipping federation of the province, proud to have worked alongside and to have become acquainted with such men—men of few pretensions who lived according to unwritten codes of fellowship that excluded petty jealousies and prejudices found elsewhere; strong men (not always big) who worked hard but played and loved as hard; men who knew their rights and fought tenaciously to keep them whole; men who ate enormous meals, drank many mugs of beer, gambled many long hours and used strong language freely but spontaneously (thus rendering poetic what in politer circles would sound obscene); but men most gentle and loyal to the little woman who came to fetch them home early on payday's afternoon, before the yielding to temptation could cause a dwindling of cheques their brows had sweated for profusely.

* * *

One night the following summer, after a hard day's work, Omoh lay reading on his couch. Transported to the world of squiredom, he saw the roguish squire walking through the fields and pausing on occasion to thwack the well-fleshed arses of the wenches bent over at their tasks. He saw their blushing faces and heard their squeals of mild surprise and protest which, however, did not conceal the delight they felt at being chosen to participate in what they knew to be a daily ritual. And then, enjoying a reader's omnipresence, he stood within a curtained chamber and watched with some trepidation a ruddy lad of princely birth (though quite unknown to him) feverishly fight his way through multi-layered clothing to reach the ample breasts of the foresaken squire's wife and pull them both full out, despite her soft protests. Omoh himself stared anxiously at the spreading blushes that threatened to destroy the virgin whiteness of the once imprisoned beauties. He longed to lay his head deep down within the furrowed space between them.

Our princely hero, on the other hand, obviously deprived of mother's love during his infancy, sought recompense by making valiant but vain efforts to swallow the one and then the other of the swollen wonders. His mistress, determined to fulfill her long suppressed maternal urges, yielded most graciously to his assaults and even urged him on with sighs and murmurings. Eventually, however, her anxiety to please the hapless youth proved almost fatal. So firmly did she hold his head against her tingling nipples that he almost expired at the very font of life.

Our prince by birth (but no means regal in his present role), apparent victim of selfish motherhood and indifferent casualty, put up a gallant struggle and, freeing himself, jumped to his feet gasping for air and coughing fitfully. But suddenly, as if to prove that he had been unarmed and meant no harm, he quickly shed his humble habiliments, revealing delightful physical endowments of regal magnitude. His mistress, touched by such spontaneous chivalry and anxious to redeem her recent excesses, strove to emulate the lad—giggling all the while. Quite frustrated by the intricacies of lace that had been woven by her ever-faithful maid, she ceased such efforts and reached out to lay her hands in reverence on the princely glory. But then (alas!) the fated lovers (the mistress doomed to never play her natural role of mother and the youth deprived of all maternal fondling) were once again crossed up by attendant circumstances.

Omoh would have warned them if he could. For he had heard the then-familiar sound of rustic hands upon soft yielding flesh, the stifled "ouches" of the startled housemaid and the loud guffawing of the rowdy squire who had surprised her at the key-hole. In fact, Omoh longed to intervene—to hold the door shut perhaps. But in such worlds, he knew quite well, the dance of life once choreographed and set in motion could not be modified, the stage once set could never be undone, the blocking once designed could not be altered. Besides, despite the privilege of omnipresence, he could not join in the cast himself nor enter in their dialogue.

No need to tell you of the sequel now. You too could travel to the land of squiredom, as Omoh did that day, if your curiosity should get the better of you. You too could be a witness of the drama there, as Omoh was, and learn what he saw afterwards and what I have decided to omit.

Eventually Omoh put down the book and turned the light off, intending to sleep immediately. But he had no such luck. Instead, he tossed and turned from side to side for several minutes, feeling himself occasionally dropping off into the dark abyss but each time waking with a start. Seeking greater comfort, he tried to roll onto his stomach, but found himself obstructed by a protuberance that he had grown accustomed to at morning times.

"But why now," he wondered to himself, "at night when I'm tired and need to get some sleep before another day of back-breaking work!"

Lying flat upon his back, he closed his eyes again and tried to make each part of his too-conscious self relax. But still he felt the surging of his blood disturb him. Then within the darkness of his firmly shut eyelids appeared (good God!) a pair of giant breasts already more than half exposed but still bulging dangerously against the flimsy garment that barely held them in. No prince himself, Omoh felt his eyes bulge frog-like (though quite firmly shut) and both his arms rise up as if to dare the much desired rescue.

Jumping to his feet, he quickly put on the lights in a desperate attempt to drive away (temporarily at least) the seductive illusion. Then as he slowly sat down, he felt a surreptitious wilting in his pants and wondered why man had been designed in such a way as to be his own embarrassment. At some times, puffed up and cocky manhood (often when desired least) and at other times (mostly when the opposite was hoped for) a shy and shrinking tendril. Always man against himself!

Omoh picked up the book he had been reading earlier and tossed it to the floor, as if to exorcize whatever evil influence it might have. Turning off the light once more, he lay down on his back as he had done before, and sure enough! he felt the hectic blood rush down to prick him up and strive to make him come alive again. Like a young rooster

78

moved by one of nature's freaks to proudly hail the dawn that lingered far off, Omoh strove to keep his calm. Besides, no phantasms of huge imprisoned breasts then reappeared.

As he lay there, he recalled that he had not touched a woman's nakedness since his arrival in the big land more than a year ago. As if to emphasize the point, a sudden throb disturbed his bulging pants-front. What's more, he thought, he had not seen Curly once during the entire summer. True enough, he had fooled around with other girls, but he had long outgrown such titillations. They surely were not proper substitutes.

The constant throbbing in his pants no longer seemed tolerable, for it became quite painful. Omoh wanted to scream out. In fact, he longed to grab the fully alerted thing and break it off!

But he remembered then how many times while lying cooing in his cradle he had felt his mother's hands (or worse! those of some quite unworthy substitute) take hold of it and gently lift it up to powder round about and after pat the "nice clean piggy-wiggy" back in place and keep it warm with soft diapers (despite the heat outside) and how afterwards each time he had reached in and twisted it all round and round then let it go and felt it slowly unwind itself back to normal shape—

how often later he had heard her yelling angrily at him to put on clothes and hide the ugly thing away from the curious eyes of mothers and their darling little girls who had come to visit and who were all surprised to find so grown a boy without a sense of privacy or shame—

how even later, after the daily ritual of peeking down the fronts of dresses at the various shapes of breasts and looking under dresses at the mysterious regions, in frustation at nights he had taken hold of it and beaten it mercilessly to tears and then next morning hated the limply hanging victim for its complicity—

how often in the peak of adolescence he had jumped out of sleep and desparately tried to stop the flood that threatened to make sleeping uncomfortable and leave betraying stains upon the sheets but all in vain—

and how finally that memorable day when he had tried to force its bruised and much abused head further through the barely ruptured hymen of his first love how frightened he had been to feel it shoot itself off prematurely and leave him (and her too) completely petrified by fear of pregnancy.

And remembering such things, Omoh felt strangely better. He no longer yearned to prune himself for, he reasoned, it was better to have wrestled with its rise and fall (erratic though it was) than not to have wrestled at all.

Soon, however, his thoughts returned to Curly, and he resolved that he would call her and speak freely to her the next day. Perhaps he would even confess his love for her and tell her of his urgent needs! Thus resolved, he immediately felt the bird of dawn rise up again with such alacrity that he was forced to grasp it lest it should fly away. Smiling proudly as it struggled fiercely to be free, he shut his eyes and, lying on his back, he fell asleep. He did not even feel himself subside within the grasp that held it still!

* * *

The next day, Omoh had to forego the luxury of eating lunch in order to fulfill his resolutions. He had to leave the ship on which he worked and hurry many blocks away to make the call. The sound of Curly's voice, however, soon made the sacrifice worthwhile. They chatted briefly about their summer holidays and would have continued longer had Omoh not espied the furtive glances of the proprietor behind the bar. Instead, he cut short the trivialities and sallied forth into his carefully outlined plan.

"Curly midear, it's been a long time since I saw you."

"Hm-m-m, that's true," the voice replied after brief reflection.

Glancing at the apparently suspicious face behind the bar, Omoh added almost in a whisper, "You see, I cannot talk much longer. I've got to return to work, and besides someone else seems to need the phone."

"Poor dear," came the reply in full contralto, "you mean you actually cut short your lunch break to telephone me."

Just then Omoh detected the impatient drum rolls of stubby fingertips on the bar nearby.

"Tell me, Curly," he managed to blurt out, "can I see you soon—t-tonight perhaps?"

"Oh my, oh my," the contralto regretted, "you cannot see me tonight. You see, I've already made some plans."

Omoh could feel a sagging in his knees, and his Adam's apple moved sharply up and down as if it were a miniature guillotine rehearsing for his execution. The dryness of his throat became unbearable. Moreover, he heard a crackling on the line and feared that they would be cut off. But with a smacking of lips, the voice resumed its melody:

"You cannot see me tonight, Omoh, but then you may see me tomorrow evening. How would you like to come up to my humble pad for dinner?"

"Why sure, sounds fantastic to me!" Omoh exclaimed almost

automatically, then added after a brief pause, "But ah—I intended to take you out somewhere."

"That's very nice of you," the voice at the other end replied in all sincerity, "and I accept—that is, for a future date. Tomorrow, I"ll expect to see you any time after seven."

Omoh could find nothing to say, but heard an hypnotising coda: "So until then, kind sir, ta ta."

Before he could reply, a sharp click and the ensuing buzzing on the line announced the conclusion of the conversation. Yet he stood there staring at the hollow mouthpiece, still holding the receiver to his ear, until he felt it roughly snatched from his hands and heard it fall upon its cradle. Only then did he observe the absence of the face behind the bar. Without turning to check, he knew who stood beside him. Startled by his discovery, he pulled his cap down on to his head and darted out through the swinging doors, not even hearing the laughter that erupted.

That afternoon Omoh worked harder than ever before, lifting bales and toting tossing catching packing parcels of all weights and sizes. Not until much later, after his arrival back home, did he feel the inevitable results of fasting while working an eight hour shift on board ship. But he did not care about such things that day. He even turned down an invitation by Kopakie (who had won at Black Jack) and Big Jay (who had received a small token of gratitude from some beautifully aging female) to go downtown that night. Soon after their departure, he turned in to sleep, exhausted and starved, expectant but somewhat afraid.

The next morning Omoh awakened bright and early, then dressed himself for work. After eating a full breakfast, he walked around the block and returned just in time to catch his ride down to the docks. Arriving there, he joined the others who waited hopefully to hear their names called and to be dispatched to their respective jobs. But Omoh himself did not care that day whether he would be called to work or not. He stared at the big clock high up above the dispatcher's cage and bemoaned its obvious reluctance to tick the minutes off.

"See how right now," he silently obseved, "the hands of time unwind themselves as slowly as a serpent overstuffed from swallowing whole some careless animal, but then tonight, if everything should chance to go all right, just you watch them dance their merry rounds of fleeting hours."

Pondering the apparent perversities of time and life itself, Omoh felt a whack upon his back and heard his name being called for the third and last time.

"He-yair, He-yair," he answered in perfect imitation of the rugged Scotsman who was his namesake and who, since that day the similarity of surnames had come to light, always reminded him that one of their two fathers must have done some travelling abroad.

"Proceed immediately to Dock C and help the others there load the hides on board ship," he heard the dispatcher announce.

"Hides!" Omoh exclaimed to no one but himself.

"You don't want the job?" the voice inquired.

"Oh sure, sure I'll take it," he quickly responded and, with a shrug of his shoulders, he proceeded on his way.

Omoh had often watched his uncle cut shoe soles of various shapes and sizes from raw leather and dip them into some mysterious liquid (which turned out to be nothing more than water) then beat them into pliancy upon his thighs with repeated hammer strokes. What's more, Omoh had never seen him wince! Omoh had also watched the older men select the thinner goat skin and clean it carefully, then stretch it out and tie it firmly over hollow rounds of wood, then warm it slowly over open fires in order to provide percussive accompaniment for unorthodox but virtuoso fiddlers—a custom and an art which the great colonial fathers in their wisdom had tried (and not too long ago) to blacken and wipe out.

But he had never visited an abattoir and so had never seen some unsuspecting animal fall gasping with astonishment at the sudden blow that cut short its life's flow. Nor had he seen its glossy coat stripped with dexterous strokes from the carcass, still warm and throbbing with vain impulses to stay alive. And he had never seen the messy skins dragged off along the ground and then hung up to dry, nor once observed the thick putrescent oozings that recently had been the very sap of life, nor smelled the stink that emanated then.

And so, one should not find it difficult to picture Omoh's disgust on entering the room in which the green hides were stored or the crawling of his skin on lifting the slippery, loosley folded bundles onto his shoulders and feeling the thick cutaneous oils seep through his shirt onto his skin.

Only then did Omoh understand the puzzled looks on the faces of his friends earlier that morning, when he had accepted the assignment without protest.

At first, he did not think that he could go on for even half an hour. The very thought of working longer threatened to relieve him of the meal he had enjoyed that morning. What had he done to deserve such punishment? he asked himself. But he could find no answer. And so, he tried to lessen his frustration by damning every animal whose hide provided man with luxuries and even necessities. In fact, he even cursed the sham that passed for beauty and for life itself. To think those ugly bloody fleshy stinking messes had once been the glossy black and white and shining brown the bulls had proudly worn! To think, moreover, that the meat he loved to eat had been in intimate proximity with such putrescent things! From that day onwards, he vowed, he would eat no meat—only fish or fowl. Perhaps he would even become a vegetarian.

Yet Omoh toiled on and on, refusing to give up the challenge of finishing the job. Perhaps, he thought eventually, such suffering was a penalty (and a just one) for knowing someone as beautiful as Curly. Besides, she had invited him to spend the evening with her. Such bliss would be sufficient recompense, indeed.

As time limped on, Omoh regretted his unwarranted hostility to the dumb beasts, who could do nothing to avoid their fate. Surely then, the culprit was man who, not satisfied with fighting to death among themselves, wreaked havoc on poor defenceless creatures. Selfish man! who to prove himself intelligent and skillful would destroy the very essence of creation. Vile man!

But Omoh remembered that he too was man and that he not only loved the animals but also loved to eat the flesh of slaughtered animals. He drank the milk that had been destined for their own young and rode upon their backs. Such things were not the idle games of catch or hunt and kill. They were, in fact, the serious business of survival.

Such thinking led to questioning and to further thinking. But there seemed to be no easy solutions. Perhaps, Omoh finally decided, one should forget such probings of life's mysteries and get on with the business of living to the full. And so, he turned his thoughts to finding better ways of carrying the hides.

Thus engaged, Omoh temporarily forgot his dinner-date with the one he most desired. In fact, he did not perceive the minutes slinking by much faster than before. Nor did he notice that the pile of hides, once so formidable, was dwindling so rapidly that the job could perhaps only last until midday. Imagine his surprise on hearing (not long afterwards) the foreman announce that they should not report back after lunch.

Omoh, to tell the truth, felt somewhat cheated and annoyed that the end should come just when he had made the necessary adaptions to the many discomforts. But he remembered with a start the appointment he must keep at all costs. He decided that he would return to the main hall, but not to seek another job. He would instead find a ride home, have a light lunch, shower, rest and then get ready for his date at leisure. Thus resolved, he smiled with satisfaction at the way in which the day had eventually turned out.

On returning to the hall after the long walk from Dock C, however, Omoh discovered to his horror that his friends had finished their assignments earlier and, thinking that he would be busy for the entire day, had already left for home. Lingering there a while, he discovered Hammal who had worked on dirty cargo at another location. With some reluctance, they finally agreed to take the city bus uptown.

Boarding the bus, Omoh, who had grown accustomed to the unpleasant odour of the hides, could not visualize how stained and grimy his clothes looked. He paid the fares for both of them and proceeded to the back of the partially filled vehicle. As he passed by the other seats, he saw the heads all turn and follow him, but he did not see the looks or scorn and anger that were etched upon them.

Hammal, by nature the shyer of the two, was no more pleasing to the eye than Omoh, but he did not smell as badly. None too happy with the prospect of sharing his tin of corned beef with five others later that day, he shuffled head down after Omoh and sat uneasily beside him.

Eventually, after several stops, Omoh understood why they had enjoyed the luxury not only of the entire back seat but also of the next two rows and of the standing room between them. Looking up, he watched the people who had recently come onto the bus walk towards them, then stop and turn sharply around to join the others packed tightly in the aisles.

Remembering a similar experience on the bus during his first year and the resolution he had made then to take advantage of such apparent adversities, Omoh stretched his legs full out in Big Jay's fashion, totally enjoying his new-found privileges. Out of the corner of his eye, he saw Hammal do the same thing, after some obvious hesitation.

Omoh could no longer contain the laughter that would not be denied and so began to chuckle. But then he heard the barly audible voice of his friend advising that perhaps they should not risk offending "the white folks" any further by laughing at them. Turning to confront the speaker, Omoh observed the trembling of his lips and blinking of his eyelids. Though moved by what he knew to be genuine concern on Hammal's part, he recognized in him an image of his earlier self. He also realized from looking at his friend's condition what he himself must look like. The superimposition of the two selves, one on the other, was a little more than he could bear with stoic equanimity. And so he let the undertone of chuckling release itself into untempered laughter, despite the many angry glances that were levelled at him.

All the way home, Omoh continued laughing sporadically, still conscious of Hammal's nervousness and somewhat puzzled by the simmering hostility of his fellow pasengers, who had been in no mood to be amused by the lighter side of life.

* * *

As Omoh turned into the narrow pathway that led to his apartment, he thought longingly of lying down and devising strategies for his encounter later on. He knew that he would be very tense and quite restrained before and after dinner, but then he hoped that after the inevitable drinks he would be sufficiently relaxed to put his plans into action. First, however, he must anticipate whatever snags he might run into in his venture. Above all, he reminded himself, he must not offend (even in the slightest way) his companion for the evening.

Just then a cacaphony of voices raised in mild dispute assailed his ears. After the immediate surprise, Omoh realized that his little room, his most humble dwelling, had been selected (in his absence) to host that day's assemblage of players. Indeed, to have one's home thus graced was always an unexpected privilege. In fact, the only greater honour was to become a member of the well-reputed group. And yet, in keeping with the selflessness of noble men who daily dealt with royalty, new aspirants were always welcome—that is, of course, provided they could meet whatever debts they might eventually incur.

Omoh himself, on several occasions, had felt the urge to join in, but after once witnessing the initiation rites he had so far satisfied himself with standing by and taking in the fascinating interplay of kings and queens and knaves and others of lesser ranks. Some day, he hoped, the treasured secrets of the age-old ceremonies would be revealed to him.

Stepping quietly down the narrow stairway, Omoh approached the door which had been left ajar for ventilation purposes. Soon he stood unnoticed upon the very threshold of the sacred arena—so recently his intimate retreat, hearing not voices but the brittle silence that prevailed and feeling the tenseness that held the several players fixed in various attitudes of expectation as Kopakie, his left hand poised upon a card face down that he must soon turn over, checked around the table to see how much he stood to lose should he go over twenty-one.

Omoh had always thought that hidden somewhere in that situation was a significant comment upon the larger game of life—specifically on the ritual of growing up and passing on beyond the well-charted realms of childhood into the dark regions of maturity. But he had never quite unveiled it and so could not attempt to give voice to it. And so, he stood there most alert but still unnoticed, watching Kopakie's left hand trembling noticeably, as if the card it lightly touched emitted ripples of a force that would soon bring the scene back to life.

Omoh saw his roommate's eyes narrowed to a fire-point and gleaming with a strange intensity, he saw his brows (like that of everyone else) glow eerily with the sweat of apprehension. For each man knew how well the turning of that card would tell whether or not he would eat bread for many days to come. Omoh himself, though not immediately involved, could hardly endure the aching stillness of the moments. Nevertheless, he knew his bread was buttered well for the fast approaching evening—and for quite a few more days to come, should everything go right.

At that very moment, a familiar figure emerged from the inner sanctum, rubbing the last wrinkles of sleep from his face. Glancing in Omoh's direction, it suddenly stopped short, throwing hands into the air and shouting,

"Oh migod! Mama look a boo-boo dey!"

All eyes immediately looked to see what presence had evoked the citing of such famous words. And soon, the brittleness within the room exploded, shattering itself and hurling fragments of laughter across the room at Omoh who, quite unmindful of the hide-stained raiments he still wore, stared stupidly around. For a while, the fragments ricochetted in all directions, leaving cheeks wet with tears and bodies limp with welcome relaxation.

Big Jay, by this time, had realized that he had committed what was tantamount to sacrilege and, as if to make amends, cried out in awe,

"Buh wha' a seeing so! Kopakie you goin' hit eighteen boy? You surely toting more than twenty-eight pounds of it."

Kopakie, who at this time needed no reminder of the implications of his decision, just wiped his brow with his trembling left hand and mumbled, "What the hell you expect me to do? You ain't see I can't beat anyone around he table."

Then casting one last longing look around, he breathed deeply and added without too much bravado,

"This way, it's do or die for me."

But Omoh, just recently the sacrificial lamb (or scapegoat, if you prefer), was thinking of men of old who dared to risk the anger of their jealous gods. To think that there could be a modern counterpart right there within the room. To think that he was privileged enough to share in such high drama. His room-mate (no Greek at all nor Anglo-Saxon either) pitted against not only six men of mortal stature but against the other Presences out there—the demi-gods, the sister Fates and Lady Luck, to name a few. Surely, he could not stand idly by! Surely, he must be the Castor to his Pollux!

And so, just as Kopakie's trembling hand approached the turned down card once more, Omoh jumped into the room and held it back, shouting to the amazement of all within the room (including him-self), "No, Kopakie! Let me do the honour."

Before Kopakie, who jealously guarded his right to "sight" his card before all others in such situations, could react, Omoh snatched up the card within his bony palm. Staring up at the ceiling with closed eyes, he slapped it face up on the table and walked head high into the other room.

The silence that persisted for a few seconds grated painfully upon his expectant ears. But just when he felt himself about to fall apart, he heard the voices once again. No cacophony that time, however, just a perfect unison rising to a full crescendo, "Jee-ee-eesus Kr-r-r-ice!"

One other sound, in whispered counterpart, spelled out a long, extended "Wh-ew-ew-ew."

Before he could move, Omoh felt himself being passionately em-braced and hoisted robustly into the air. Kopakie, who usually could hardly spare the energy to become emotional, seemed temporarily endowed with super strength, as he carried Omoh bodily out into the others too, despite their recent setback, picked up the scent. Omoh himself, still throbbing with the thrill of recent success, detected the disturbing odour. But it was Big Jay, who was nearest to him, that first was scattered on the table.

"The Vice Squad rides again," he lyrically announced. "Well lads, that's it. So endeth the lesson. We'll welcome you another t—"

But the sentence was never concluded. Big Jay, still bent over at his task, suddenly turned his head and sniffed the air, like some proud hun-ter sensing the proximity of some long-sought prey or enemy. The others too, despite their recent setback, picked up the scent, Omoh himself, still throbbing with the thrill of recent sucess, detected the dis-turbing odour. But it was Big Jay, who was nearest to him, that first took action. Dropping all the gathered coins back onto the table, he bolted for the doorway, at the same time pushing Omoh firmly aside. Soon the entire pack, goaded by their protective instinct, followed close behind out through the open door.

Somewhat dazed, Omoh stood surveying the room in which he had been left alone. The cards, recently alive with meaning, seemed sadly inert there upon the table. The pot of silver, so hotly contested mo-ments ago, lay scattered there apparently unwanted. It all seemed so ordinary then. But strangely enough, the scent persisted. Needless to say, Omoh soon realized his plight. The odour that had caused the rapid exit—the very one that held him motionless—was no other than his very own. On one hand, he thought, he was still haunted by the lingering smell of death but, on the other, he still bore upon his shoulders the burden of man's struggle for survival.

By that time the players (except Kopakie, of course) had dispersed. Broken by the recent turn of events, they had seized upon the opportunity of Big Jay's scamper through the door to leave not only the room but also the entire scene of action. Soon Big Jay himself, holding to his eyes a bright red handkerchief polka-dotted with black spots, returned with Kopakie following closely behind.

"Christ Omoh!" he exclaimed, "you fall into a sewer or what? Or did someone bless you with a shower from a bedroom window?"

"No man," Omoh answered tiredly, "Just those damned hides— the green hides I worked on this morning."

"Hides!" came the echo, in perfect unison.

"You mean you worked on hides?" inquired Big Jay with a gesture of amazement.

Then assuming a more familiar role, he continued in a rather soothing tone of voice, "Nah man, Omoh. You should mark 'No hides or wheat' on your disc, man. One smells too bad and the other goin' choke you to death eventually."

Still turning his head from side to side as if to emphasize his point, he paused for a while, then added, "Long after the job finished, in the first case, you smelling stinker than old salt-fish and, in the other case, you blowing wheat-dust from you nostrils and coughing it up too."

While Big Jay spoke such words of advice to Omoh, Kopakie quietly collected his winnings with hands that still trembled. But as Big Jay grew silent, he added in his usual undertone,

"Anyhow Omoh ole boy, stink or sweet, you not only turned up a winner, but you got rid of the opposition just in time. A don't think miluck would've held out much longer."

Big Jay, glancing mischievously at Kopakie, winked at Omoh and proclaimed, "Tonight's the night! It's gonna be a big one." Then hearing no immediate response, he added with a grin, "Eh Kopakie, boy?"

"Ha ha," Kopakie chuckled softly, 'Maybe I could afford enough to buy a bottle. But if we goin' to celebrate, we must get some company. How about the big blonde, Omoh? Think she's available?"

"My God!" Omoh exclaimed, not worrying to answer. "What the hell is the time?"

Without waiting for an answer, he rushed out through the door towards the makeshift bathroom, leaving in his wake the several pieces of his offensive attire. Totally puzzled, Kopakie looked inquiringly at Big Jay. The latter slowly shook his head from side to side, then lifted his right index finger to his temple and turned it round and round in circles, as if to say, "The guy's gone loco, man."

* * *

After a careful but hurried shower, Omoh realized that he had not brought a change of clothes with him. And so, very much against his liking, he resolved to chance the journey back to his room in total undress. Holding his flimsy towel against his shrunken pendulum, he rushed across the dimly lit basement. But (alas!) the door that had been left ajar all day long was closed and (much worse!) it would not yield to either tugs or jerks. Resorting to the use of both hands, Omoh could feel with every pull the precious seconds beat themselves against his thighs.

Finally acknowledging that he had been deliberately locked out, he was about to bang loudly against the door when he restrained himself. What if the noise should bring Miss Banard downstairs to make inquiries? How could he possibly explain his standing there all naked? Those bloody asses! He hoped they were having fun.

At this point, Omoh decided to stand there silently and wait to see how long his friends would carry on their childish game. But after several minutes, he began to wonder if perchance they had decided to go out and had accidentally locked the door behind them. In his desperation, he turned and took firm hold of the doorknob, then yanked the blasted thing with all his strength.

To his surprise, the door, as if someone had summoned its immediate release, flew open, sending him stumbling backwards in a most awkward fashion across the open space. After crashing heavily against the stairway, Omoh thought of grabbing something solid and bludgeoning the guffawing pair to death. And perhaps he would have made at least a gesture of so doing had he not heard the soft pattering of feet approaching the door immediately above him and the creaking of a bolt being hastily withdrawn.

Instead, he picked himself up and darted headlong through the open door into the inner sanctum where Kopakie and Big Jay lay doubled up with suppressed laughter on the bed. Grabbing the nearest pair of pants, Omoh put them on just in time to hear Miss Banard's soft voice inquiring if everything was all right. Coming out to the outer room, Omoh saw her standing pale and obviously quite agitated at the door that he had not thought of shutting.

"Oh yes," he managed to answer with surprising equanimity. "I just slipped and fell against the bathroom door."

Not really convinced but much relieved to find him unhurt, Miss Banard could only say, "Thank God," then turn and make her way back up the stairs to sojourn once again within the tropic regions of her dreamworld.

Omoh was angry at the others, not so much for tricking him but rather for causing Miss Banard to make an unnecessary trip downstairs. He turned sharply and stamped into the inner room, intent on bitterly chastising them with his narrow serpent's tongue.

But as he turned the corner, he happened to observe himself within the tarnished mirror. The sternest resolutions could not have stemmed the laughter that the image of himself dressed up in Kopakie's baggy pants aroused. And so, what could have been a nasty scene resolved itself into five minutes or more of belly-aching fun. Someone of philosophic bent could easily have found there a vivid rendering of life's absurdity, for the tears that came to Miss Banard's eyes while listening to them were not the tears of joy.

* * *

For some time after that, Omoh could not find the freedom to ponder his upcoming dinner date. Although the honoured players had long ago departed, he could not yet reclaim the privacy of his room. Not only was he conned into revealing the well-kept secret of his invitation, but he was also forced to sit and listen to his friends, Big Jay and Kopakie, compare their recent day's activities.

Any other day, such a happening would have been more than welcome entertainment. But Omoh wanted very much to be left alone then. True enough, he could no longer hope to sleep a while before his departure, but he must formulate some plans and then rehearse them several times within his mind. Instead, he sat there and listened to his pals, not even comprehending what he heard nor taking note of any fascinating details. Eventually, however, his reluctance to participate gave way to a curiosity that would not be denied. And soon, he was completely drawn into the dialogue. In fact, he was even moved to tell his own experiences.

With subtle modulations of his voice accompanied by the requisite gesticulations, Omoh narrated the entire drama of his mornings activities. The effect of his performance was far greater than he had anticipated. As he reached the climax of the bus ride with Hammal, Big Jay, who never could repress a healthy laugh, was forced to make full use of his polka-dotted handkerchief. Kopakie, though always concerned with keeping whole his stock of energy for serious sleeping later on, laughed with no less fervour. But whereas Big Jay often pirouetted off the bed with surprising agility, Kopakie always kept his seat.

Right after the laughter had died down, Omoh heard Big Jay announce that he must take his leave. Big Jay, who never kept a woman waiting (not even those to whom he had explained his reluctance to kiss as stemming from his early religious training), had agreed to meet with "a friend of a good friend" later that evening. And so he had to get home to do his exercises and rest up for a couple hours. Indeed, it was his custom to prepare himself at all times for whatever services he might be called upon to render. Only in that way could he maintain the good name he had established among the charitable ladies.

As Big Jay got up to leave, Kopakie pulled himself up into the middle of the bed and lay there comfortably curled up. Smiling with happy anticipation of imminent repose, he waved a limp goodbye to Big Jay. Omoh, anxious to be left alone, followed Big Jay up the narrow stairway out into the street where the big blue Nash stood ready to roll on to new adventures. He seemed to be making sure that Big Jay was really going home.

With familiar coughs and gurgles, the well-travelled car aroused itself and slowly moved away. Waving a hasty farewell, Omoh turned and hurried back to reclaim his room at long last. Peeking into the other room, he saw Kopakie stretched out diagonally across the bed and betraying on his face a serenity that comes only with deep sleep.

Omoh shed everything but his underpants (the lone veteran of his first year) and let himself fall heavily on the bumpy couch. Stretching himself fully out, he tried hard to relax, but soon gave up the effort. Then as he realized how little time he had for preparation, he began to contemplate alternative approaches. "Let's see," he whispered to himself, "should I resort to truth and candor—the tried and proven way, according to my mother and others of the older generation? Or should I employ subterfuge and guile in the manner of more modern strategists? Should I assume the role of someone lovelorn and desperately daring and so risk the hazards of impulsiveness and fearless confrontation? Or should I instead play the shy and hesitant young man, a victim of enchantment, and so try to move the Circe's heart through pleasantries and subtleties to compassion and subsequent compliance?"

Instead of longed-for solutions and restfulness, however, new complications continually revealed themselves to him. Most disturbing was the simple fact that he himself, an alien from the Rock of little international significance, was on the verge of trying to possess someone belonging to the big land he had always dreamed about.

Omoh heard faint voices from the past inquiring what he would choose to be if he were privileged to be born again. He heard as well the unmistakeable reply of his closest childhood companion—the sturdy looking lad who had long ceased to walk on earth and had not yet found elsewhere the secret of being born again (that is, as far as we could tell). He heard him speak of being born again in the person of a screen star, like Clark Gable or Charles Boyer, for only then (he argued) could his dream of coming close to the blonde beauties of the big lands somewhere out there ever be fulfilled.

Omoh, at that time, had been confined within the aura of his own fantastic speculations but, now for the first time, he understood the yearnings of his friend. In fact, he would have been delighted if some enchanted lips had kissed his froggy self into some princely presence worthy of the adoration of the lovely Curly. Such lips, however, if they ever existed once upon a time, had long since fled in terror of uncivil times and perhaps dwelled only within the haven of the fairy tale.

Omoh then felt a strange longing to escape the world around him that seemed so enigmatic. As he lay there confounded by uncertainty, he recalled the many times he had lain in bed back home while myriad insects chirped their varied harmonies and visualized himself as the world's most talented musician. He remembered too the many times that he had listened to the early morning birds vie with each other for lyrical supremacy and painted pictures of himself as an admired writer of romantic verse.

For the first time, however, such nostalgia did not comfort him. Instead, it aroused strong feelings of guilt and shame. For the first time too, Omoh had to confront the tragic paradox within which he himself, like all his childhood friends who dreamed of being born again as millionaires, fast-shooting cowboys and such, had long been trapped. And so, eventually, he began to understand that while they had flourished in the tropic fullness of their world they had moulded their dreams out of the stuff of distant lands. Their images of happiness were never garnered from the life they knew and thrived upon. For, well-conditioned by the glamour and the glitter of the world of cinema and books, they always shaped their fantasies in borrowed forms. Even the stubby prickly trees decked out to welcome Father Christmas were always arrayed with fluffs of cotton wool to simulate the snow they never knew and never could experience.

* * *

No longer ashamed but restless still, Omoh decided to get up and begin to dress. Consulting the loudly ticking clock on Kopakie's cluttered desk, he discovered (much to his surprise) that barely a quarter of an hour had elapsed during what had seemed to be at least a long hour's meditation. Since he wished to look his best, however, he proceeded with the greatest care to select the items of attire he considered most suitable for the occasion. Afterwards, he meticulously combed the hair that had been recently cut short and, to keep the stubborn pepper grains in place, he put upon his head the upper section of a stocking he had cut in two and knotted in the middle. Finally, with unusual circumspection, he put on the chosen garments. All the while, he kept in mind the observations that his mother would have made on similar occasions during his youth.

Despite Omoh's deliberation, the ritual of getting himself ready was finished more than an hour before the intended moment of departure. He thought of sitting down a while but decided not to risk wrinkling his pants. He told himself, in fact, that pottering about the house would only increase the chances of getting his clothes soiled. The only smart thing to do, he therefore concluded, would be to leave right then and, instead of travelling by bus as was his wont, to walk to Curly's place. He would take his time and so be able to observe the area which he had not visited before.

Omoh thought of awakening Kopakie to get his opinion of how he looked. But the image of an angry creature prematurely aroused from hibernation loomed large before him, causing him to change his mind. And so he went to the mirror to check himself in case there was something amiss. To his astonishment, he there beheld a bald-headed figure staring out at him with large bulging eyes. Trying not to think of what he would have suffered had he gone out into the street with the stocking on his head, he pulled off the horrid thing and patted all the ruffled spots back into place.

Soon after, he walked through the door and shut it softly behind him. With some trepidation, he walked up the narrow stairs out toward the front of the building. And such would have been his attitude through the entire journey had Miss Banard (enjoying one of her rare visits to the verandah) not called out to him, "My my, don't we ever look smart today! She must be quite a beauty, Omoh, to deserve all this." Then, with a sigh so soft that Omoh never heard it, she added with all sincerity, "Enjoy it while you can, young man. Life's too precious to be wasted."

Omoh looked up in time to see the crippled figure shuffle off through the half-open door into the haven of her dimely lit room. He wanted very much to speak some words of gratitude to her, but he could think of nothing quite appropriate. And so he continued out into the street, carefully wiping away the lonely tear about to make its mark upon his lightly powdered face and remembering that he had not kissed Ma Poppo, Janice nor Mildred on the day of his departure from the Rock.

* * *

Omoh walked along the pavement at an easy pace, observing the varied patterns on its multi-fractured surface and trying (without hopping-scotch) to set foot only in the spaces. Not far away from the house in which he lived, he almost bumped into a couple headed for a nearby Hungarian restaurant. After awkward apologies and uncomfortable glances, they all continued on their respective ways.

Well well, thought Omoh with a look of mischief in his eyes, so Popsie really got something going with the island queen. And to think that Black Boy had been saying so all along and nobody believed him—despite his reputation. He couldn't wait to give Sir Free the lowdown. Black Boy, in fact, was something of a mystery. He seemed to know the ins and outs of everybody's life, although he spent most of his time locked up in his apartment.

Omoh remembered visiting him very early one morning and listening to him tell in full detail all that had happened at a dance the night before. What was most astounding was the fact that he had not left his house that night and certainly had not had the opportunity to speak with anyone before Omoh's arrival—for Black Boy did not have a telephone. He, indeed enjoyed only those luxuries that cost him little or nothing. As he himself so beautifully worded his philosophy of life, he smoked and drank "any given amount" of cigarettes and food and Scotch.

Omoh had never spoken to Popsie before that day, but he had heard a lot about him. Popsie, it was proclaimed, never drank, smoked or cursed. Sometimes, however, he could be moved by one of his many female admirers to fool around a little. Popsie, you, see, had won his distinction not only as a scholar but as a sportsman as well. No wonder he was well-respected on and off the campus. He seemed, moreover, to be one of those rare people who succeeded at almost anything they tried. Besides, he always did it his own way. Popsie, in fact, had been involved in many an unusual situation. On one occasion, he had caused a mini crisis among the big-wigs of the sports administration. After winning several awards in cricket and athletics, he had dared to be outstanding in football (or soccer, as they call it in the big land). But since there was a limit to the number of awards any one person could win in any given year, he was debarred from further distinction.

Well, my friends, there was such a to-do as a result of that decision, with charges of discrimination flying here and there, that a special committee had to be set up to deal with the unprecedented situation. No need to tell you how it eventually turned out.

At other times, however, things had not resolved themselves as favorably for Popsie. One year, as captain of the Varsity A cricket team, he had watched his opening bowlers (or pitchers, as some would call them) mow down most of the opposition for less than a quarter of the runs they had been set to make. Then, to the surprise of everyone, he removed the then-successful bowlers and replaced them with two spinners! Soon the fields resounded with loud shouts of protest (which soon turned to boos and hisses) as the tail-end batsmen settled in and steadily built up their score. When Popsie finally elected to bring back the disenchanted pace bowlers, it was much too late. The match was lost! Without any delay, his enemies (mostly those friends of his who always envied him) sought their revenge. Within a few days' time a meeting, which until then had been almost impossible to set up, was held and Popsie was demoted from the captaincy.

Omoh himself had been annoyed that day to see a captain give away a game his men had played so hard to win. But afterwards, especially after hearing Popsie's explanation of his apparently irrational behaviour, he firmly disagreed with the team's decision. The spinners, it seemed, had not come out to practices, and Popsie thought it fit to take advantage of the big lead to give them a workout. Omoh, in fact, thought that Popsie was worth much more than the whole damned bunch of chicken-heads.

Thinking such things, Omoh walked on to meet the lovely Curly. At one point of the journey, he neglected a red-light and almost walked into the oncoming traffic. Pulling himself sharply to a halt, he looked around to see if anyone (besides the drivers of the passing cars) had observed the near disaster. To his relief, there seemed to be no one around at that moment. But he realized that he was still within familiar territory. And since there was still quite a long way to go, he decided to increase the tempo of his walking—but not enough to cause him to perspire freely.

And the island queen! Omoh chuckled to himself, tickled by the memory of his own experiences with the famous lady and her subjects. He recalled the popular complaint among them (and among the already coupled men) that their male counterparts preferred to take out native girls—that is, the daughters of the pale-faced conquerers. Omoh himself, just after his arrival in the big land, had felt the same way. In fact, he had accused his friends, on several occasions, of abandoning their own girls. And he did not change his views even when it was pointed out to him that there were over fifteen boys to every island girl. Instead, he openly expressed his skepticism for the many stories told of how those very girls had taken full advantage of the disproportion. Had he a charger then and a coat of mail, he would have set himself up as a champion of the much abused sex—as a genuine black prince.

At that time, the island queen herself seemed to have detected something special about Omoh. During the classes that they both attended, she always sat next to him and, if he happened to be late, she kept the seat beside her free for him. In light of all this, Omoh had chosen to neglect the fact that each day, at the sounding of the buzzer, she quickly gathered up her books and hurried from the room to meet a group of islanders he did not know. What's more, she had never seen fit to introduce him to them. Instead, whenever he passed by, she always seemed too busy chatting to observe him.

Eventually one day, Omoh walked by the happy-talking group, trying to attract the island queen's attention, but without being too obvious about it. As before, however, she did not once look in his direction. Somewhat disgruntled, he hurried around the corner as if he hoped to flee his own embarrassment. But alas! he found himself right in the middle of another gathering. As he looked around inquiringly, he saw projected just beneath his nose a crooked but familiar finger. Then, in like manner, other straighter fingers all around him found their mark while faces, frozen and unsmiling looked on attentively. Standing there with a stupid grin upon his face, Omoh eventually found the courage to ask, "What the hell are you all staring at?"

Immediately the strained silence exploded into laughter all around. But no one answered him.

"Now what the ass all you laughing at?" he fired at them, this time speaking much more loudly.

The only answer he received, however, was a heightening of the laughter. Even more confused, he surreptitiously examined his attire to see if there was anything out of place. But he discovered no such thing.

It was Sir Free who then explained the reason for the scene. Realizing that what had been good fun was fast deteriorating into pointless cruelty, he had withdrawn the famous finger and stilled the laughter with an upraised hand. The night before, he then revealed, Olga, the island queen, had vigorously denied all suggestions that she had a crush on Omoh. In fact, she had topped it off by loudly exclaiming, "Me! Me, in love with he? Y-y-you mus' be mad. That p-p-picky-head, s-s-sissy man!"

Then before it could have been pointed out to her that everyone within the dining hall had heard her, she had continued with obvious contempt for all men such as Omoh, "Migod oh! M-m-me in love with Omoh! And dey have s-so many g-g-good-looking brown skin m-men around. And with straight hair, b-b-besides."

Quite surprised, Omoh watched the group disperse itself as each man hurried on to meet his separate appointment. Forgetting all the things that he himself had meant to do after his class, he walked around in circles while reminiscences from a more remote past assailed his mind.

Omoh had not been born on the Rock from which he had departed for the big land, but on a smaller island not too far away. There he had lived among a people who were almost all of African descent. In fact, he knew the names of every East Indian family who then resided there and the names of those few whites who had fled the harsher climates of their native lands in search of tropic comforts. But Omoh had never once envied their lot. Instead, he had always taken pride in being (as he then thought) a true native of the land and, consequently, one of its rightful owners.

After he was forced to travel to the Rock, however, to live with Ma Poppo, he had soon discovered that he was "a small islander" and, for that reason alone, fated to enjoy a lesser life (at least, on earth). What's more, he also realized then that only those of fairer skin could hope to be employed by banks and private enterprise. And he learned that, among the darker shaded ones, only those few who had studied abroad and later won themselves distinction as professionals could dare to ask for membership in private clubs or seek accommodation in luxury hotels.

In fact, Omoh soon understood why the very girls who had flirted openly with him during their vacation in the smaller island passed him by as if he were invisible. But at that time, he had never dreamed that one as dark-complexioned as himself would one day reject him on account of trifling physical details, such as the shade (not colour even) of his skin and texture of his hair! Especially when the people of the big land (being mostly white) observed no such distinctions.

* * *

Thinking such things, Omoh walked on to meet his Curly at a slightly faster pace. Fascinated by the recollections of his island past, he temporarily forgot the island queen and his relationship to her. But soon the image of himself walking about in circles returned to haunt him.

That was the very day, he then reflected, that he had begun to understand and to appreciate the preference of his fellow islanders for the native girls. Soon afterwards, he had found himself admiring and indeed respecting the fair creatures who daily ran the risk of being ostracized by friends and families alike, of suffering harassment at the hands of cops and others in authority, and of being persecuted by the island girls. All on behalf of the strange dark men they loved (or believed they loved).

Just then, the face of one such heroine flashed itself before his eyes—she who had dared to take the un-fair hand of some young intern from the islands in holy matrimony. Her parents (of course!) had adamantly refused to grace the ceremony with their presence or even (in their absence) to give their blessings to the determined couple. How could they, indeed, knowing that they would be cursed with mongoloid grandchildren? But Omoh also recalled the obvious remorse of those very parents, after they had chanced to see the healthy bronze-complexioned scions of the union. And too, the many precious gifts and vast sums of money they had offered in atonement to the much-abused young husband of the once-rejected daughter. Omoh, in fact, still did not believe that he himself could have had the bigness of heart to forget and forgive as they had done.

Thinking such things, Omoh proceeded at an even faster pace to meet his Curly. Already he began to feel a difference in the atmosphere. Along the avenue, tall evergreens that scanned the furthest regions of the city from up high cast their multi-foliated shadows on the sidewalks. And golden streaks of cloud along the far horizon bestowed a softness to the pleasant twilight scene. Neither the soft purrings of the passing cars nor the slightly louder rumbling of the city buses could disturb the stillness that seemed to calm the nerves.

Fascinated by the new environment, Omoh paused a little while. He lifted his head as if he meant to do homage to divine presences above and breathed deeply inwards, feeling the healthy rush of air far down within his breast. All around him beneath the smokeless chimneys and antlered television antennae, grey silent houses, surrounded by unbroken hedges of luxuriant growth, displayed a studied similarity of shapes and sizes. Through the windows, soft light from gilded chandeliers poured upon rectangles of thick lawn, casting a bluish tint upon the well-trimmed surfaces. Only a silhouette or two against the curtains, already drawn against the world outside, betrayed the lives within.

Moving slowly onwards, Omoh could have sworn that he heard the happy laughter of children frolicking about the fairy-land of coloured lawns. But they were nowhere to be seen. The doors were tightly shut

98

against the wicked witches who might ride their broom-mobiles up from the city slums. Safe within their castles, they had nothing to fear— except perhaps the villains and the monsters of television worlds.

Just at that moment, Omoh felt the flush of mild embarrassment grow warm within his cheeks, for he had somehow recalled the small two room basement where his daily life was spent. Was it possible that he would one day enjoy the comforts and protection of such homes as he then saw? Surely the chill of wintry nights and days could never trespass upon the thickly carpetted floors within those curtained halls. No greasy grimy walls there, nor dingy blotchy ceilings. No lingering food smells, nor broken mirrors on the walls. No wonder, he thought, the children of that world (the fairest of them all) performed so brilliantly at university. What a difference it would make if he could find a room for rent around there. But the thrill of such surmising did not last for long—it ended just as suddenly as it had begun. For Omoh knew that even if there should be such a room he could not affort it. Besides, the ones in charge would never rent it to him. For Omoh was familiar with the problems of renting apartments in the alien city.

On one occasion Big Jay had selected an address from the official list of rooms available and had visited the home. There he was politely greeted by the master of the house and questioned as to the purpose of his coming. After he had stated his interest in renting the apartment, the man before him explained that he had nothing at all to do with such affairs. Just then, a woman, obviously his wife, inquired in a voice that bristled with authority, "Herman! Who is it? Who is it, Herman?"

"Just some student interested in the room downstairs, dear," the husband answered nervously.

"Then why didn't you call me before? You know that you are not capable of dealing with such things."

Nodding his head in apparent agreement, the hulk of a husband shrugged his shoulders and walked away as a woman, no more than five feet and one hundred pounds, came rushing to the door amidst a clatter of falling pots and pans.

"You could tidy up the kitchen and dry the dishes meanwhile, Herman," she suggested rather firmly as she handed a wet towel to the dejected figure passing by.

"Well, hello there!" she greeted Big Jay, somewhat succeeding in controlling her surprise at seeing him standing there, mopping his brow with a black and yellow polka-dotted handkerchief. Anyone within earshot would certainly have thought that they were old acquaintances. Big Jay, who always preferred to do business with a woman, bowed gracefully. With a glint of mischief in his eyes, he answered

99

with a lilt, "Good day, milady. Is your mother at home?"

The woman, for a moment, seemed to be entranced. Her mouth, already opened to play the part she had so carefully rehearsed for such occasions, remained wide open. Regaining her composure, she smoothed her hair and smiled.

"How flattering you are, young man," she cooed. "I am the only mother and wife within this house."

"Oh—oh!" lamented Big Jay. "I'm very sorry. No offence intended, Ma'am."

"Come come, my boy," the other scolded, "no need to be apologetic," still trying to smooth the hair that was already rolled up tight in curlers.

Looking over her head into the house, Big Jay checked to see if the husband had been listening. At the same time, he reached into his pocket for the official list of rooms available, then pointed to the underlined address.

"I got your number from this list, and since I was in the vicinity I took the opportunity to drop by to see if the room was still available," he explained.

As the other tried to modify her script to suit the scene that had not proceeded as she had expected, he then added, "I know that I should have phoned first and I am sorry for not doing so."

"Remember now, no apologies," the other reminded him. "One must make hay while the sun shines, you know."

"Well put," observed Big Jay, "that's very true. They also say that the earliest bird always gets the worm."

"Ha ha," laughed the other, quite forgetting the purpose at hand. "You funny man!"

No sooner had the words come out of her mouth than her hands reached up as if to block them. Perhaps she realized that he was indeed a funny-looking man. Or she could have suddenly detected that she was being conned. Regardless, she immediately pulled her face together, completely destroying the girlish smile that had lingered there a while. And then, the funny-looking woman, returning to a more familiar routine, explained the reasons why she could not rent the room to Big Jay. She was forthright, indeed, but always most polite.

The problem was his colour. Oh no! She had no prejudices. But in their world, which was totally screwed up, people were funny (again reaching up too late to block that word out)—unpredictable. Why, she was sure that her neighbours, with whom she did not have a close relationship but with whom she was forced to maintain some contact, would never forgive her for taking him in. They would think that she had gone completely overboard (pointing to her head, all rolled up tight with curlers). They would crucify her! They would even stoop so low as to accuse her of having an affair with him! By the way, she did not mean to imply that he was not good enough for her (looking up full into his eyes). In fact, her lousy good-for-nothing husband (leaning closer and speaking almost in a whisper) would be the first to start the rumour. He had been trying for a long time, but without success, to take revenge on her. And for no other reason but that she was the smarter of the two. Imagine that! (watching Big Jay nodding obvious sympathy). Just for being smarter! (more sympathetic nodding).

"And better looking too," Big Jay interjected, struggling all the while to fight off the laughter that threatened to possess him.

"Funny ma—funny you should say that," the other began but soon rephrased.

"Well," said Big Jay, trying to spare her any further embarrassment, "I understand—I know the world is full of funny people. But it is always good to learn that there are still some good ones too."

The blush she had so far managed to suppress immediately tinged her cheeks, but with disastrous effects. No healthy glow appeared there. Instead, a deep yellow tint put in relief the tensions, frustrations and anxieties that were etched upon her face.

For just a while, she seemed to feel the emptiness of all she treasured in her life. Not smiling, she looked down upon the dampened apron that she wore.

Big Jay then bade her goodbye, speaking quite softly as if to calm whatever emotions she might be suffering. And as he turned to go, he added, "I'm really sorry, Ma'am. I'm sure that living here would have been quite in-ter-res-ting."

As if those words had freed her from some magic spell, she called aloud to him,

"Hey! Just a minute, young man. I think I may be able to help you." Then turning to confront her husband, who happened to be just emerging from the kitchen, she cried out, "Herman, got a pencil? Or a pen, Herman?"

But Herman, not seeming to hear her (or perhaps not caring to), shuffled right past her into another room. Seeing that, Big Jay decided that it was time to quit the scene. But first, quite overcome by curiosity, he called softly to her, "Here, Ma'am," and offered her a pen.

Accepting it, she turned and reached for a notepad on a nearby table. Then she scribbled on a page she had dislodged, folded it neatly in two and handed it to Big Jay, together with his pen.

Not long after, when Big Jay was seated in the more familiar confines of the big blue Nash, he stretched his legs full out, started the motor and listened to the engine warm itself against the chilly air. Soon, as he urged the faithful companion into motion, he turned to look once more at the house that had almost become his temporary home. And then he saw (or thought he saw) the pale outline of a hand waving to him behind a frosted window. But he soon dismissed the idea as the idle workings of his imagination.

As he turned the corner, Big Jay remembered the neatly folded piece of paper within the pocket of his overcoat. Perhaps, he thought, he should check out the apartment the woman had suggested before going to the old place where he had lived for three years. As he searched for it, he could not understand the logic of her actions. Why should she send him to a friend's house, knowing full well what would be in store for him? Perhaps she had actually told him the truth about her neighbours. Imagine that!

With extreme caution, Big Jay smoothed out the then-crumpled piece of paper against the steering wheel. He saw not numbers but words written in bold print. But he put off reading it until he came to a stop sign nearby. Taking advantage of the fact that there were no cars immediately behind him, he once again smoothed out the crumpled paper and read:

IT COULD NOT BE HELPED! SUCH IS THE WORLD TODAY BUT IF YOU CARE TO CALL ME SOME DAY (YOU HAVE THE NUMBER)—YOU FUNNY MAN YOU!

SMILES

Despite Omoh's awareness of Big Jay's trustworthiness, he had found it quite difficult to believe his story. And perhaps he would have (for the first time) deemed it completely fabricated, had not he himself been privileged to see and read the neat but boldly written script upon the crumpled paper. Big Jay never told him whether he had called again or not.

Afterwards, Omoh had heard reports of similar experiences from his other friends. Each time the woman of the house (not always small) had to be consulted, for the apartment was her special project. Omoh, in fact, remembered thinking once that some day, if things continued as they were, the men might form a liberation movement. Most of the time, moreover, the woman's lines were well-rehearsed but always spoken with politeness and apparent sincerity. And most of the time too, the neighbours proved to be the culprits on account of whom the rooms could not be rented to the dark strange men—funny men from far away.

On one occasion, there had been an unexpected modification of the dialogue. The woman of the house, being all alone, had loudly proclaimed her liking for the lad. In fact, she openly confessed that if she were younger (with rapid fluttering eyelids) she would not hesitate to go out on a date with him. Her problem was not with the neighbours nor with her husband (he was quite older than she and besides he never stayed at home). You see, she had three daughters, two of whom were adolescents. And with such a charming young man around the house, who knew what would happen? They would almost surely become enamoured of him. And (don't forget it) that would be allright, had they been older and as experienced as their mother. For then they would have been prepared and strong enough (like her) to face the ugly reactions of her friends and others to her choice of male companion—a choice that was only natural, he being so utterly good looking and mascu-line!

Unlike Big Jay, who thrived on such situations, the lad in question was quite dumbfounded. All he could do eventually was to mutter apologies and shift his weight from foot to foot. Just before he left, however, he found the courage to accept the slender hand offered to him in kind farewell. He felt a tingling within him as it closed firmly upon his own and held for a while with steadily increasing pressure. So completely enthralled was he by the unexpected turn of events, that he hardly heard her whisper, "You know, if I were younger and much better looking, I would accept your invitation to meet with you."

And before the startled youth could point out that he had made no such request of her, she added, with faster fluttering eyes, "But no, my love," placing her hand upon her breast in the fashion of the queens of silent screens, "Fate, cruel Fate, would not let it be. Go go, my lad, make merry while you may."

The lad to whom these words had been addressed just barely heard them for, noticing the pallor of the face and the trembling of the hands, he hurried down the stairs into the streets before she could fall into a faint.

* * *

Caught up in the landslide of the past upon his consciousness, Omoh had unwittingly slowed down his pace of walking. He also recalled the efforts he himself and friends had made to cope with those well-meaning but much too timid souls whose names were listed under "Rooms Available". He remembered how his fellow-islanders had paired themselves with others from the big land and walked around throughout the city centre. The native sons (more than welcome prospects) would check to make sure that an apartment was still vacant and then send their island partners to request accommodation. If they were turned down or told that they had come too late, the owners were confronted and then notified of the deletion of their names from the official list. At first the project proved to be effective, but eventually the guilty ones began to advertise in the dailies and in notices put up outside their homes.

Soon a persistent rumbling and grumbling of Omoh's stomach attested to the fact that he was getting hungry. Besides, he must not keep his lady waiting. And so, proceeding once again at a much brisker pace, he hurried on to meet his Curly. Not long afterwards, Omoh realized that he was fast approaching the address he had been given. With each step he felt more out of place. He thought that he had heard the sound of footsteps immediately behind him, but soon recognized instead the heavy pounding of his heart. The few people he encountered on the way all seemed to turn their heads as if to question his intrusion upon their private world. Yet nothing could deter our anxious hero from his destination.

Each successive cross-street took on added significance, for Omoh knew that he must soon turn off the avenue onto the alley on which the doorway to his fair one's home looked out. With an eagle scout's alertness he found the unpaved roadway (as wide as or wider than the major streets back on the Rock) on both sides of which gateways, almost identical in shape and size, invited passersby to enter into well-lit homes through well-attended squares of gardens.

Somewhat flustered, Omoh walked slowly along trying to decide which of the many gates (the fourth and fifth along the right side?) he should approach. After some delay, he decided to investigate a number painted in small figures on the nearest doorway. But as he leaned against the railing to improve his vision, a sudden vicious barking disturbed the silence of the evening. And soon, a monstrous creature came bounding towards him.

Startled, Omoh withdrew in terror to the other side of the roadway. To add to his dismay, a figure of immense girth appeared within the opposite gateway, wildly gesticulating and crying out in fierce contention with the barking monster. Omoh could not tell whether the person was a man or woman, until he heard her say, "You men are all alike. Every single night since I hired Thelma, a different one of you keep coming to my gate. Well, either you get to hell out of here or she goin' t'get her walking papers, now."

Not quite believing what he had just heard, Omoh instinctively retreated toward the lesser danger of the barking Husky.

"Thelma! you know that man?" he heard the giantess inquire.

And then, a timid voice replied in a familiar accent, "No Ma'am, and a not expectin' no one t'night." Then after a pause, "Besides, 'im far too dress up fuh me!"

"Well, you better be careful, girl. One more of these night prowlers and bam!" (striking her fist against the palm of the other hand) "I goin' send you packing."

"But ma'am, ah downt—" the other started to protest.

But Omoh could no longer hear her words above the screaming youngsters who had rushed out to put their arms around the distressed maid. The children, it seemed, could not bear the thought of Thelma being sent away. No wonder, thought Omoh. Who would wish to live alone with such a horrid creature?

Moving carefully along the right railing, Omoh began to make his way down the alleyway. But then he thought he heard the chuckling of a familiar voice above the fast-fading barking of the Husky. And then, beyond a doubt, a siren voice called out amidst the suppressed laughter.

"Omoh, where are you going, dear?"

Turning sharply around, Omoh discerned the unmistakable outline of Curly standing there beside the monstrous guardian of the gate, not barking then but whimpering softly beneath her lightly stroking hands.

"Oh—oh," Omoh mumbled, at a loss for words, "I—I couldn't see the numbers on the doors, And then that monst—"

"Oh him!" she interrupted. "He's just an overgrown baby—completely harmless."

But Omoh was not reassured. No Heracles himself, he cautiously approached the gateway that would lead him to his paradise.

"Come on, Omoh," Curly urged him on, "let's go inside," turning to lead the way.

"O.K.," he answered, still keeping his eyes upon the lingering canine.

Finally convinced that it was too preoccupied with its departing mistress to take notice of him, Omoh softly pushed the gate, entered quietly and replaced the latch. But as he lifted his head, a shaggy blur appeared in the corner of his eyes. He felt himself drift backwards and, with a thud, bump heavily against the gate he had just shut. Struggling to regain his balance, he felt a weight against his chest and then the slimy slurping of a huge smooth tongue upon his cheeks. Omoh thought that he would die, so firmly was he pinned against the gate. The odour from the slurping mouth was anything but pleasant. But soon the siren voice ended the nightmare.

"Down! you silly boy. Get down!"

Omoh was sure that he had detected an unexpected hardness in the voice, but he soon dismissed the thought. Reaching for the collar on the dog, Curly pulled the monster off and sent it to its kennel with a sharp rebuke.

"Sorry Omoh," she apologized, trying at the same time to brush away the imprint of the Husky's paws.

"Oh no!" Omoh softly moaned in his dismay on seeing the smudge on his jacket. "Not after all the care I took this afternoon."

Then hanging his head dejectedly, he followed Curly on through an obviously abandoned flower garden into the house. ·

* * *

"Please take off your jacket and give it to me," Curly requested of her dinner guest. "And make yourself at home, dear," she added.

As she left to wash away the offending paw marks, Omoh walked into the sitting room and looked about him. Something about the place—something that seemed to speak aloud about its owner—strove to impress itself upon him.

Against the far wall, an open piano, the obvious heritage of many generations, proudly displayed its bulk upon huge wooden talons. On a stand above the keys reclined a number of old manuscripts and music books. The complex notations on the overlapping well-worn pages were barely legible. And two gilded candlesticks that jutted out on either side were stuffed full with prematurely butted cigarettes.

From the piano top and in a four-tiered bookshelf, a disarray of magazines and books assailed the eyes. A shrubbery of variegated markers sprouted from within their dog-eared leaves. In the corner to the left, a faded canvas stood askew on a crooked easel. A pair of arms painted on it seemed to be pleading desperately for the quick completion of the body. Other paintings in various stages of completion were stacked on a nearby chair and propped against the wall. Such things and many more Omoh observed, standing in the sitting-room. But still he could not (or perhaps refused to) articulate the message that he received from them. Eventually, he sat down upon a thick-cushioned sofa—another antique piece.

Just then Curly reappeared, with a familiar pixie smile upon her face.

"Your jacket's all clean now, but just a little wet," she assured Omoh. "I hung it to dry."

Then with a practised tossing of her frisky curls, she went on to inquire, 'Tell me, Omoh, were you at some meeting or formal ceremony just before you came here?"

For the first time that evening, Omoh noticed just how casually (or rather, scantily) Curly herself was dressed. After a brief but awkward silence, he replied, "Oh no. Just thought I'd put on my best—though it's not much to look at—for you, milady."

"Well well! That's very *galant* of you, my dear. But really, you shouldn't have." Then moving closer to him, she patted him on the head, lightly ruffling the hair that he had stocking-groomed so carefully.

"What would you have to drink?" she cooed at him, apparently hoping to soothe his obviously hurt feelings.

"Whatever poison you have to offer," Omoh responded, doing his best to loosen up.

"Well, there's gin," she explained, holding up one finger, "and scotch and vodka and sherry and wine—wine for dinner, of course," she continued, adding another finger with each item.

Then, as he sat trying to select one item from the suggested variety, she added with a little cry, "Oh! I almost forgot! I bought some rum especially for you—your favourite island drink."

Omoh felt trapped. He strongly suspected that it was not island rum, but some other local stuff he had once tasted and strongly disliked. But he could not refuse something that was supposed to be a special gift.

"Here comes your rum and Coca Cola," he heard her sing out in a good imitation of the Andrews Sisters' version of the calypso. Omoh remembered, with great satisfaction, that they have been sued and forced to pay a healthy sum to the original composer of the song. Too bad he drank himself to death soon afterwards, he thought.

Curly, humming and moving to the rhythm all the while, went into the kitchen, but soon reappeared and handed him a glass full of "rum and Coca Cola".

"Take off your shoes and loosen up your tie, Omoh," she advised. "Come, sit over here and relax—here where I can see you while I check a few things in the kitchen."

Moving over to the designated chair, Omoh flopped into it and let himself sink in deeply. Sighing with relief, he anxiously took off the shoes that had not been quite broken in before his walk that afternoon and loosened his tie—but only a little. Sitting there with glass in hand, he smelled the heavy molasses of the thick native rum. God! how he hated the sickly sweet concoction! And to make it worse, she had mixed it with another drink he loathed. Only the bloody Yankees and a few never-see-come-see islanders mixed their rum like that.

Omoh then heard voices—voices from the distant past of childhood—reminding him that honesty was always the best policy. He wished to tell the truth to Curly. But he heard another voice—a much more recent voice—explaining that the rum had recently been bought especially for him. And so, as he had done so many times within the past year, he recognized the inevitability of sometimes overruling those voices from the past of childhood. Never could he hurt his loved one's feelings! Surely he, if anyone, must be the one to suffer.

Omoh lifted up the glass and, calling out to Curly, "Here's to your health, milove," he downed a little more than half the drink without a pause. Determined to surrender everything to the success of the evening, he put down the glass upon a nearby coffee table and let himself relax deep in the comfortable chair.

Omoh and Curly then began to talk. They talked of every little thing that was of mutual interest to them. He reported on his recent activities, picking up the conversation right where he had left it off the day before over the telephone. He spoke with gusto of his experiences, as a longshoreman, he spoke with obvious pride about his contributions to the success of the Varsity B cricket team, but he spoke with quite restraint about the music he had played at various dances, nightclubs and jazz concerts.

She, in turn, responded to his enquiries with monosyllables or brief nonchalant phrases. Teaching the year before had been "as usual", her relatives were "well—considering the circumstances," her painting and her piano-playing had been "neglected of late", and her love-life—" whatever *that* was supposed to be"—was "just as it was the night you met me, Omoh." Life that summer (and indeed before that too) seemed to have been completely uneventful, as far as Curly was concerned.

Omoh could not believe that. Someone as beautiful as Curly should never suffer a dull moment. Like the rose itself, she should attract the busy hum of life to her immediate environment. All living things, in fact, should come to her to sip the life-force that she generated. The only thing that she had managed to achieve that summer, she eventually admitted, was to get a good tan—by no means a perfect one. Of course, she still had far to go to be as dark-complexioned as he was. Omoh felt a pin-prick of self-consciousness somewhere deep within him and cast his eyes down to the floor before him. But soon a strong yearning to regard the well-tanned body of his lady possessed him, quite restoring him. How strange! Up until then, he had not really noticed it, so preoccupied he must have been with other things.

And so he lifted up his eyes—but slowly, very slowly. They fell upon her ankles and lingered there a while, then (with a sigh) perceived her slender legs and travelled up along their lengths to where, above the slightly dimpled knees, they (with some trepidation) watched the gradual expansion into firm shapely golden brown thighs that disappeared beneath a short, tight-fitting skirt. Then (becoming bolder) they traced, without the slightest difficulty, the blue-shadowed outlines that rose and merged into the mysterious V, the alpha and omega of all human life, and blossomed into the figure eight of well-fleshed loaves of arse, narrow waistline and much broader shoulders.

Omoh felt a hotness and an itch beneath the collar of his shirt. His tie, already somewhat loosened, rubbed against his restless Adam's apple. He pulled it further down and undid the topmost buttons of his shirt. Reaching for his glass, he looked around the room taking note (once again) of the many details. To his surprise, however, they had gone strangely silent.

"The potatoes are almost done now," the siren-voice intruded upon the silence, breaking the mystery of the moment.

"Aha, that's good," the spellbound victim answered automatically.

But further speech became impossible. A sudden pounding of his heart had forced a gushing of his blood to his head, holding his mouth agape and his eyes bulging frog-like. Meanwhile, the room, lurching crazily, had hurled itself into a sudden swirl of motion, threatening vertigo. Omoh, however, soon recovered, forestalling any possible embarrassment.

As he had turned around in response to the siren-voice, he had seen before him a sight that he had frequently enjoyed in dreams, but never thought that he would have the privilege to witness in reality.

There before him, just within his reach, stooped his fair enchantress, attending to the contents of the oven. Her soft bosom, now exposed, had swollen into two well-moulded jellos of flesh just where, minutes ago, her swan-like neck had disappeared into a loose-fitting blouse. The well-tanned golden-brown faded gradually and dissolved itself into a creamy hue which, touched by the wonder of the transformation, grew warm and, blushing, resolved itself into a silhouette of nipples.

Staring speechless, Omoh watched the breasts which, though they had already suckled a woman-child into full life, had preserved their girlhood firmness and resilience. He watched in trepidation, for he feared they might force apart the buttons that just barely held them in.

"My God," he thought, "they are more beautiful in the reality of flesh than in my dreams."

In his confusion, Omoh barely realized that the object of his admiration had just spoken to him, but he had not heard the question. And so he stammered,

"So—sorry dear, wha-what did you ask? I think I was ah—daydreaming for a while there."

Smiling coyly, Curly cooed at him, "Oh really now! that's interesting, rather in-ter-res-ting."

As he wriggled in his seat and gulped down the rest of his drink, she calmly explained, "I was just observing that perhaps I ought to put the steaks on soon."

Steaks! Wow! My gosh! Omoh silently exclaimed. He had seen the thick red cuts of beef so often in the supermarkets and the local butcher shops. But he could never afford them. And even if he could have bought one, he would not have known how to prepare it.

"My my, Curly," he suggested in all sincerity, "you should not have gone to all that trouble—I mean, you should not have wasted all that money on me."

"Well," the siren-voice smiled at him, "what's done already's done, me dear. Enjoy yourself, it's later than you think."

Omoh picked up his glass to drink to Curly's health once more, but he had already drained it of its contents. Curly, however, noticed and promptly apologized,

"Gee, I'm sorry, Omoh. Your glass is empty, I should have filled it up before." Then stopping in her tracks, she turned around and called out to him, "Why don't you help yourself, dear."

Though quite ashamed to have been caught in an act of obvious avarice, Omoh rose at her suggestion and entered the kitchen beside her and began to pour himself a drink.

"One for you too, dear?" he softly inquired.

"Why not?" the lilting sing-song answered.

Turning to take her glass, Omoh watched with some surprise as she finished off the drink that she had hardly touched in one uninterrupted swallow.

"Tell me, my dear," she started as she handed him the glass, "how would you like your steak done?"

Wha—a—?" Omoh countered with another question, thinking at the same time, "My God! if she doesn't know how to prepare the damn things, how could she expect me to know?"

"Well done, medium or rare?" he heard the siren-voice continue.

"Ah well, let's see" he answered bravely, stalling for time. Obviously, his thoughts continued, she knows not one way of doing steaks, but three! "Why rare, of course," he spoke out without knowing why.

"Rare meat done by a rare woman in a rare manner," he added in spontaneous eulogy.

Returning to his seat, Omoh watched with interest as Curly moved about the kitchen with grace and confidence. He saw the healthy-looking steaks, heard the sizzling of the oil that sealed the juices in, and smelled the rich odours that made his mouth fill prematurely with saliva.

Boy oh boy, he gloated to himself. How very much unlike the accustomed smell of stewed chicken that prevailed within his room. He felt like singing out loud! Perhaps, since he had long lost the voice he once possessed, he should play the piano instead. But no, he counselled himself, one thing at a time, repeating another of the many maxims that had been drilled into him during early childhood. And so, he quietly sipped the rum that he had poured into the glass—this time, however, without the Cocoa Cola. To keep the secret from his lady, he had filled the glass up to the previous level.

Smacking his lips after the second gulp, he loudly announced, "My, this *is* good rum" believing it himself. "Not bad at all."

"I knew you'd love it, dear," he heard the lyrical response. "That's why I bought it for you."

Omoh felt his spirits sag a little. He hated deliberate deception at all times but, more than ever before, he hated his performance at that very moment. Once again, however, the evening was saved. He heard the siren-voice, more lyrical than ever, suggest,

"You better polish off that drink, young man. Dinner's almost ready."

"Okay," Omoh sang out in feigned contralto. As he lifted the glass, he somewhat dreaded the possible results of downing so much of the rum he actually disliked.

Yet, as Curly approached him, he put the glass to his mouth and tossed the contents off. As he struggled vainly not to grimace, he heard the lady say, "The honour's your, kind sir, to open up the wine."

* * *

Seated at the table from which Curly had just removed a miscellany of bills and books, purses and pennies, hats hairpins mascara and such things, Omoh admired the hand-embroidered linen cloth that she had spread upon it. How many times, in days gone by, had he observed such finery being fashioned by his mother's fingers. How often had he watched the purple shuttle, that he himself had wound tight with special thread, fly in and out the petalled loops like busy hummingbirds at work. The spinner, meanwhile, had kept up a steady stream of conversation with her friends and students, laughing heartily and pausing only to carefully unravel some prematurely tightened knot. How many other times, while studying not far away, had he listened to the pleasant monotone of clicking needles (knit one purl two) and turned at intervals to note the slow but steady evolution of the intended product.

Omoh himself had dared to risk his father's wrath and worse by leaving off the urgent pursuit of his academic grail to practice (horror of horrors) at the distaff—a much more fascinating thing! Despite the frequent humilitation suffered at his father's hands, he had managed to complete (under his mother's guidance) a pair of bathing trunks. The jealous gods, unfortunately, had seen it fit to lay bare and deflate the subsequent vainglory of our hero.

On that fateful day, Omoh proudly displayed his handiwork before a group of friends that he had gathered on the beach for that particular occasion. After a calculated delay, during which time he happily acknowledged their compliments and congratulations, Omoh, with a loud cry, rushed into the surf and plunged headlong into the onrushing ocean water. The crowd, mostly composed of budding-breasted girls, stopped their cheering and watched with anxious glances here and there for him to reappear. Omoh, meanwhile, despite the aching of his screaming lungs, prolonged his underwater swimming. At the last possible moment he bounded flying-fish-like up to the surface, desperately seeking the precious air above.

Alas! Omoh, in the ecstasy of creativity, had forgotten to make the necessary compensations for the stretching of wool. And so, the sigh of great relief that welcomed his long-delayed emergence had hardly spent itself before a muffled cry was heard among the spectators. Then silence! Silence that soon erupted into waves of raucous laughter.

For there before them they had just beheld a dark and fragile figure, the object of their recent adoration, rise up in all his nakedness, gasping for air. But then they watched him dispppear beneath the swollen surface once again and reappear, waist deep much farther out to sea.

The clattering of plates being put upon the table dispelled the vivid replay of his past embarrassment. Smiling to himslef, Omoh watched Curly as she brought out the steaming vegetables, the hot potatoes topped with butter within their silvery wrappings and, finally, the steaks still sizzling lightly on oven heated plates.

"Why don't you pour the wine," he heard her say. "I'm sure you're starved by now—I myself could eat a whale right at this very moment."

Omoh waiting until she had turned again to fetch some other item from the kitchen, quickly pushed the lower quarter of the cork that he had managed to break in two into the bottle and then filled the glasses. Keeping for himself the glass in which the brown fragments danced about, he placed the other next to his lady's plate.

"Boy, does that ever look superb!" he then exclaimed. "And does it ever smell good.!" he added, swallowing hard.

"Did you call me 'boy'?" Curly inquired with a look of mischief on her pixie face.

"Ah—what? Me call you b-boy?" Omoh stammered."I guess I did. But you know," he quickly added, "I could never mistake you for a boy—never. Boy—ah—I mean, Curly, that would be impossible."

"Oh, I just wondered," Curly chuckled at him. Then coming to the table, she continued with some apparent concern, "Let's hope it tastes as well as you say it looks and smells."

She then sat down, picked up the glass of wine and chanted, "Here's to your health. Cheers and long life to you."

"Best of all to you," countered our gallant one. "May all your dreams come true."

"Even the nightmares?" she asked, still smiling mischievously. But before he could find an answer, she suggested in another tone of voice, "Okay okay, let's dig in while its hot."

At the instant, she picked up her knife and fork and approached her steak. Omoh felt relieved that he had not been called upon to say grace. before the meal. He was sure that he would not have been able ro remember the lines had he parroted each and every day during his island schooldays. In fact, he never really understood the meaning of the sounds that he had uttered then.

Sitting there at table, he believed that nothing could deprive him of a perfect evening. The wine was good—not sickly sweet like the bloody rum and Coca Cola, nor tongue-tying like the extra-dry white wine he had one time tasted but had a hard time swallowing. The steak itself looked so inviting that he would try the other things, the potatoes and the vegetables, before surprising his unaccustomed palate with a delight so rare.

The potatoes first. Ah man! so good so good. Some wine to wash it down, And then the vegetables. Delightful, so very delightful. Some wine again, but just a little sip. Mmm-mm-mm. And now—

Picking up his knife, Omoh noted its partly serrated edge and heartily approved the wisdom of such a device. For on several occasions, he had struggled long and valiantly with stubborn chunks of stewed beef. Turning his plate full circle, he lightly touched the dark brown

113

surface several times as if in awe. Finally succumbing to the urgings of his agitated stomach, he pushed the fork full into the tender meat and, without pausing, began to cut with greatest care a neat square from the steak,

For a while, Omoh stared in disbelief as the bright pink of the severed portion slowly grew red with oozings of its blood. What could have gone wrong? Cooked beautifully on the outside, but completely raw on the inside! Perhaps Curly in her anxiety to feed him had not allowed the steaks to fry sufficiently.

"Something's wrong, Omoh?" he heard her ask, not realizing that she had been observing him. Taken aback, he looked up and saw that she had eaten freely of the other steak, which had been cooked no more than his.

"Oh no. Just thinking how very lucky I am to know someone like you," he somehow managed to extemporize.

Then picking up the square of meat he had just cut off, he placed it in his mouth and chewed upon it. To his surprise, it was quite delicious.

"Good, really good," he commented, meaning what he said.

Ignoring as much as possible the freely flowing redness, Omoh kept eating for some minutes. Buttered potatoe first, some vegetables next, potato once again, and then a small piece of steak. And with every other mouthful, a sip of wine to bolster up his spirits.

But try as he might, Omoh could not blot out the intrusive redness that oozed with every cut. And soon (woe upon woe) an oozing of another kind appeared to add to his discomfort. He shivered as bright images of hides, thick green hides dripping with putrescent sub-cutaneous oils, superimposed themselves upon the reality of bleeding flesh before him. Immediately, a queasiness within his stomach threatened (once again) to embarass him. At that very moment, the resolution that he had made and broken earlier that day—the resolution to become a vegetarian—seemed most justifiable.

But, as so often before, a timely intervention on his lady's part forestalled the threatening nightmare. "Omoh what's wrong?" he heard her ask again. Only that time, he heard (or thought he heard) that touch of hardness he had earlier perceived but had dispelled as false.

"Is your steak not rare enough? Or are you feelling ill?"

No longer able to disguise the truth, Omoh confessed that he was troubled by the rawness of the meat—but only on the inside! The rest of it, he hastened to explain, was sufficiently well done.

At that instant, one would have certainly expected Curly to rebuke him for playing games. Had she not given him the choice of having his steak well done, medium or rare? And had he not expressed his preference for having it done rare? But she seemed to understand the situation. For resorting to her previous lyricism, she inquired whether he would like to have his steak cooked a little better.

Somewhere in Omoh's mind, the unpleasant montage of bleeding steaks and slimy dripping hides still lingered. But he could not deny the gnawing hunger that he then endured.

"That would be very nice, my dear," he answered with poorly feigned nonchalance. "But I don't want to cause you all that trouble. Besides, your steak will soon be cold.

Recognizing the futility of making any response (it seemed), Curly got up, picked up his plate and took it to the kitchen. Sitting there alone at the table, Omoh felt tired and quite shaken. Just when everything seemed to be going well, the worst had happened. Looking across the table, he saw that Curly had already eaten the greater portion of her steak. He felt a little better. A least, her meal would not be ruined by the interruption.

"Pour yourself some wine. There is a little left," she suggested as she walked back to the table. To his dismay, however, she only paused there long enough to gather up the remnents of her meal. Turning right around, she took it all into the kitchen where she finished it while attending to his steak.

But soon, all doubts and questionings were completely allayed as Curly returned with his own steaming steak upon the platter. No need to tell you all the details of the dinner after that. Suffice it to say that Omoh thoroughly enjoyed his well done steak and then dessert and liqueurs aterwards. Curly, meanwhile, finished her dessert, drank several after dinner drinks and listened to her guest apologize one minute for his stupidity and then, within the next, pay tribute to her cooking and obvious tolerance.

* * *

After dinner, Omoh sat himself down once more into the old comfortable chair from which he watched her moving about the kitchen, returning bottled condiments to their accustomed places and stacking high within the sink the dishes, pots and pans that she had used. Sipping from another glass of rum and Coca Cola that she had mixed for him, he thought that he would further indulge his appetite by feasting upon the scantily clad beauties of his tanned one. And so, he watched her as she removed the spoons, the knives and the forks from the table, then put away the beautifully embroidered linen tablecloth.

Returning to the kitchen, she paused a while to contemplate the pile of dirty dishes. But after a few minutes' hesitation, she took a flowered apron from a nearby drawer and put it on. Pulling on a pair of rubber gloves, she turned and, with a familiar tossing of her head, began to wash and rinse the stacked utensils.

Omoh, despite the comfort that he felt, aroused himself and called out to her, "Let me do the drying while you wash, dear."

"That's nice of you, Omoh," he heard her soft reply, "but I am afraid the size and setup of my kitchen will not permit such happy arrangements."

And then she added with a chuckle, "Just sit and rest yourself. Remember that you told me all about the siesta you generally take right after eating."

"Ha ha," laughed Omoh with all his island unrestraint. "The Mexicans! they have their siesta. We from the Rock! we suffer from plain and ordinary niggeritis."

"What's that?" cried Curly, temporarily interrupting her task. "Nig-nigger what?" For a while she seemed to think that she had said the wrong thing.

"Niggeritis, my dear—the inevitable and irresistable urge to flake right out after eating," he explained with some exuberance. "But not for long—just for a half hour or so." Remembering Kopakie's unrivalled performances, he quickly added, "That is, where most people are concerned. There are a few exceptions."

"Anyhow, whatever it may be," Curly retorted, "sit down and relax yourself. I'll soon be finished here."

Omoh immediately relaxed deep in the old chair. He let his head fall backwards into a comfortable position, but soon twisted himself around to improve his vision of the lady. That time, as he watched her, he felt no itchings nor other discomforts of the neck or Adam's apple. Instead, he felt his blood play truant and rush down to meet a summoning more urgent than digestion. Omoh enjoyed the throbbing and the tingling that he then experienced. In fact, he urged them on by giving free rein to his imagination—already much too fertile. Despite such pleasant sensations, however, he could not ward off for very long the drowsiness that accompanied the sweet contentment of a well-filled stomach. And so, he soon felt his eyelids, much heavier than before, threaten to black out the image of the one he dearly loved (or so he thought).

And then came sleep—deep sleep, deep peaceful sleep—somewhat like a drug, only it doesn't stupefy—and then a band of angels, coming—coming for to carry—coming. . .

* * *

That night, after the dinner about which I have just told you, Omoh dreamed a dream that he had dreamed some time before. Only this time, the images—though slightly modified—appeared to be more vivid than the previous ones which, in fact, had been so vivid than that he had all but failed to recognize the unwelcome intrusion of reality.

Floating upon a gentle gust of wind, Omoh felt himself being wafted on within a liquid sunlife. And all around, he felt the freshness of the air that tasted of some distant ocean-home. But then, a sudden failing of the breezes made him fall free—not speedily, but with a strange sensation of something being unexpectedly retracted from deep down within his stomach. Almost weightless then, he rolled over twice, head over heels, and landed on a green cushion of thick grass. Spurred on by curiosity, he soon got up and, with light bounding steps, hurried onwards deep within the land—his lotus land where nothing seemed to be imperfect or disturbing. At last, though still unwearied (for nothing seemed to warrant effort there), he let himself sink slowly down upon a hillock where stood a solitary tree.

And for a long time, he sat there alone, relishing the honey of contentment *and* listening to the perfect harmony of sounds in soft andante, tingling with the feather strokes of restorative breezes and breathing in the fragrance of the balmy atmosphere, while gazing steadfastly at the undulations of green-cushioned land that stretched beyond his vision.

But then the taste of sweet contentment soon began to cloy, the chorus of sounds still blended in full harmony became increasingly monotonous, the healthy breezes lacking the immunity of mild contamination gradually began to wane, the fragrance of the atmosphere grew faint beneath the pressure of its own necessity, and there before his eyes the cushion of land dissolved itself into a restless bog of mushy green that threatened to engulf him. In desperation, he felt the urge to cry out. But there was no one close by to hear him and come to his assistance. Besides, the cry itself seemed to be frozen by the chill of indolence somewhere deep within him. And so, he felt his helpless self being slowly tossed and rolled about by grey-green swells that seemed to leer at him with strangely human countenances.

In the panic of the moment, Omoh did not feel soft hands take hold of him and raise him up with unexpected firmness. Nor did he feel himself being led away into another land, until he heard a distant siren-voice assuring him that he would feel better soon. Just then indeed, he also perceived a figure next to him, above whose dimly outlined form a

117

circle of gold seemed to be glowing halo-like against the dark. And (once again) Omoh recognized the presence of his lady who always, at the most ill-fated moments, came to his assistance.

His feet, no longer struggling beneath unsteady knees, fell more firmly on more solid ground. But soon his legs, already fragile, made painful contact with an obstacle that he had not observed. At that very moment, Omoh felt the guiding hands let go of him, allowing him to drop quite unexpectedly upon a quilted surface. Afraid to move, he lay prostrate for some time, observing the dark nothingness before his eyes. Somehow the unsteady motion that he had recently experienced persisted. In fact, it seemed to worsen with each passing moment. Like some stowaway deep within an ocean liner's womb, Omoh could feel impending nausea. The very darkness seemed to grow more thick. The air itself, thick with the scent of perfumes, unwashed underwear and sweaty garments, made breathing almost impossible. He knew that he could not resist regurgitation much longer.

But then, exactly at that point when self-control seemed about to come apart, a pleasant voice not far away brought welcome relief to Omoh. The very siren-voice that recently had reassured him came rippling into the stifling darkness, escorted by the bolder sounds of piano accompaniment. Fascinated, Omoh recognized the lyrics (somewhat gushing) that he himself had heard so many times and learned by heart during wartime days. No longer claustrophobic, he let himself relax. But yet, as if entranced, he kept to the spot where he had fallen earlier. Relieved, he observed the recently oppressive darkness slowly take on a lighter hue and felt the restlessness within him rocked to sleep upon the gentle lilting of the bewitching tremolo.

Smiling as he listened, Omoh gradually reconstituted the events of the recent past. Surely, he must have totally succumbed, as he had done so many times before, to an attack of niggeritis. Then, after a while, he must have suffered quite severely the ill effects of overeating and drinking much too much. Especially that bloody rum and Coke! That's why he felt so sick a few minutes ago.

But where the hell was he? The last thing he remembered clearly was sitting in a large old chair, watching Curly wash the dishes.

Moving for the first time (but only slightly), Omoh reached out his hands and realized that he was lying on a bed. Oh hell! that's it, he thought. That must be her dressing table there—there where he could just barely discern the bottles of perfume, the boxes of powder and kleenexes, the oils and lotions that were supposed to make one beautiful, and other items of her toilet. And there, upon the bed-head and on that chair—in fact, scattered everywhere!—were various pieces of her clothes—her dresses, panties, brassieres and other things, the names of which he did not know for sure.

"My God!" eventual comprehension moved him to think. "You mean to tell me that I was so deeply asleep that Curly brought me all the way here into her bedroom without my realizing it! Boy, what an ass am I! After all that planning and careful preparation, I fell asleep at the wrong moment—just when the woman's warm and full of drink. To think of all I must have missed! Wow! That gal must be as strong as a mule. True enough, I am a featherweight. But sleeping weight is dead weight, man, and that is plenty weight. Pappayo, I must have been really tossing and turning in my sleep out there. Hope I didn't do anything really embarrassing—like dribbling or vomiting!"

Wiping his mouth with the back of his hand to make sure that he had not embarrassed himself, Omoh raised himself up on his elbow. He could not recall seeing a bedroom when he first came in. But then the attack by that monstrous canine had so upset him that he could have easily missed it. Anyhow, here he was. What should he do? Why indeed had she brought him there? Why hadn't she awakened him and sent him home or given him some coffee or some tea or something else for his upset stomach?

He then thought that since he was awake and feeling better, he should perhaps go out and sit with Curly. And then perhaps they could sing together, play duets and spend a real romantic evening. But what if she should decide to send him home as soon as he went out? He surely would not be happy then. In fact, he could not even stand the thought of it. What should he do, then?

Just then Omoh remembered a story told to him by Big Jay. In fact, it was not a story, but a detailed account of one of his many escapades. One time, it seemed, a woman whom Big Jay greatly admired—and, of course, desired with a burning passion—proved to be much more of a problem than he had anticipated. Were he convinced that her reluctance to comply was founded on the tenets of an old-time Puritanism (which seemed to have most of the country in its rigid grasp), he would have graciously withdrawn from the relationship. But realizing instead that she was only being coy, our man persisted— not pressuring the lady by any means, but just biding his time until the propitious hour.

That day (rather, that evening), Big Jay, somewhat like Omoh earlier, had been invited to dine with the desired one. After the meal, they both had several drinks and chatted amiably for a while. But soon after, she rejected his mild advances—not roughly, but tactfully enough to keep him off without driving him away. Big Jay, however, had decided that the long-awaited moment had arrived. When she excused herself to wash the dishes, he stretched himself full out upon the couch, which he knew was really a bed-sitter. Soon, as he was about to let himself doze off, she reappeared and asked him to stand up until she pulled the bed full out. Smiling surreptitiously, Big Jay immediately obeyed. Eventually, she wished him a happy nap and left him alone once more.

But Big Jay had never intended to take a nap. And so, even though she tried repeatedly to awaken him (for it was getting late and he should leave before the landlady got mad), he prolonged his sleep— a sleep well punctuated with well-practised snores. Finally, she ceased her valiant efforts to arouse him and took pity on the exhausted young man, who obviously had spent most of the night before reading those heavy volumes. Needless to say, she soon lay down beside him (for she herself was a hard-working woman). Proud of herself for having eventually decided to risk the ire of the nosy woman who managed the apartment block and so appease some of the guilt she felt about the young man's heritage, she soon relaxed into a happy slumber. Further details were quite unnecessary, for the smile that broke upon the hirsute face that told the story bespoke the happy early morning sequel. Which proved, as Big Jay succinctly put it, that oftentimes duplicity resulted in long-desired harmony.

Shaking his head as he had done in Big Jay's presence the day he heard the story, Omoh resolved to try a similar routine. And so, slackening his belt a bit, he let himself relax and waited for the inevitable moment of Curly's return. In fact, if nothing else, he might enjoy a night of comfortable sleep upon a queen-sized bed.

Listening to the tremolo of Curly's voice, Omoh realized more fully the talents she possessed. Her piano playing was not bad at all, considering the fact that she had not practised for a long time. Such natural gifts, he thought, should never be neglected. As he thought of Curly sitting there all alone, however, Omoh could hardly resist the urge to go out and play the part he had so often seen performed by Gable, Boyer and such men. But he had already decided to emulate another master—one closer to him and one whose victories were won upon the stage of everyday life and not within the prescribed world of cinema.

And so he lay there propped up on one elbow and silently breathed in the hot and heavy scents of women's luxuries, not feeling nauseous then but somewhat light-headed and pleasantly intoxicated. Looking about the room, he paid careful attention to those pieces of clothing that had recently enjoyed proximity to the well-tanned flesh he had been privileged to gaze upon.

Omoh, indeed, could almost feel the mind-blowing hotness of that flesh and almost taste the sweet salinity of the thick dark-shadowed nipples. Turning slightly to relieve the aching arm on which he lay, he felt the sudden softness of a silken garment right there against his cheek. At that instant, the coolness of the thing blazed to a pin-point that hurled him bolt upright with heavy-pounding heart and wildly pulsing blood. He thought that he would soon black out!

But (once again) the magic of the siren-voice prevailed, quite calming him and lulling him down into peace and comfort upon the quilted surface. As he lay there, he let himself succumb completely to the essence of the moment. Closing his eyes, he watched the dark red spangles of the blackness perform their rhythmic movements and listened to the measured progress of the notes that touched him, hypnotic-like, inspiring the sweet surrender of all tensions and anxieties to nothingness and pure passivity. And then sleep, deep sleep, deep peaceful sleep—and a band of angels coming—coming for to—for to carry—to carry—to . . .

* * *

Thinking, "My God, I fell asleep again!" and then, "but only for a short while, thank God," and trying all the while to meet the unexpected turn of events with calm control and circumspection, Omoh lay still on the very spot where he had earlier passed out. Not feeling the quilted surface as before but instead an unaccustomed softness and a coolness, he tried to still the myriad questionings that whispered in his head.

Thinking, "What the Hell's going on?" yet not too anxious to discover what the answer was (for fear of not being capable of coping), Omoh thought of shifting slightly to ease the burden of uncertainty that seemed about to crush him. But all effort proved to be in vain, for something held him mummy-like within its tight constricting bonds. Feeling the unpleasant grating of his Adam's apple against the dryness of his throat and the uncomfortable bulging of his frog-like eyes, Omoh could hardly fight off the urge to cry out loudly against the restrictive darkness. Any moment, he thought, and the frailness of his body would certainly break down.

Back on the Rock, Omoh would have known for sure which of the villagers had carefully stripped off his veil of skin and, shrinking into a blazing ball of fire, had winged aloft in search of blood and fallen upon him. But in the big land, he could never entertain the possibility of such evil presences. Perhaps, he hoped, it was all a dream or (at worst) a visitation by the legendary night mare. Where then the good lady of the siren-voice? Oh that she might come to rescue him!

As if in answer to the silent prayer, Omoh soon felt an easing of the pressure on him. And then a rustle! and a sigh! so soft that he perceived them almost without hearing them. At that very moment, an unwelcome coolness sent warming shivers up and down his spine, which instantaneously curved forward puppet-like and pulled his knees high up, foetus-like, into the hollowness of stomach.

But then a sudden contact jolted him straight out again, igniting a shock of recognition. Omoh could not believe it! He seemed to doubt the very things that reason and the senses strongly recommended. My God! How could she have done that? And without waking him again! Surely he had only slept about half an hour. How could she? And why would she? My God!

A swarm of possibilities invaded Omoh's consciousness. Too many to hold still and then choose the only fertile one. In the silence of the dark, the awesome pounding of his heart threatened to disrupt the temporary calm. The hectic blood-beats seemed anxious to run out their measured course and merge into the inevitable still-point. Try as he might, he could not restrain them.

After a few uncomfortable minutes, Omoh carefully reached out to readjust the light covering so as to keep out the cool night air that entered freely through a window (left half-open) on to his naked body. In the then familiar darkness, he discerned the various items of his clothing strewn upon a nearby chair. The ticking a nearby watch (just barely audible) seemed to announce the rapid coming of the dawn.

What should he do? How fast asleep was she? Or was she actually awake, but feigning sleep to see what he would do? If so, would she gladly welcome possible advances? Or—or would she, shocked by the rudeness of a hopeless ingrate, loudly protest and—and send him packing out into the chilly night? What's even worse, should the monstrous canine then arouse the neighbourhood, would she deny her friendship with him and label him a peeping Tom?

Just then, a distant chiming of a clock three times surprised him with the revelation that he had slept not half an hour but closer to four hours! Impossible! How could that be? Not long ago he lay there and listened to her singing the very songs he knew.

Come come, a calmer self alerted him, it only means that there is little time left to act. Here you are in all your birthday glory (for you have reason to be proud, though skinny!) and there, so close that you could actually enjoy the latent fires of her naked body, the woman that you burn for.

Christ! He could not stand it! He would go mad soon! What would Big Jay have done in such a situation? Too bad he omitted the details of his early morning triumph. Too bad, indeed.

Omoh no longer felt the chilly night winds. Instead, he trembled as the surge of passion wrestled deep in him with icy doubts and fears. Bound upon a wrack of indecision, he lay paralysed, feeling a strong aching in his heart. Alas! no magic wand appeared to touch him into action.

The chiming of the quarter hour (though soft) quite startled him. The sound itself, wafted from afar upon the gentle breezes of the night, loudly impressed upon him the folly of his procrastination. Across the wide screen of his consciousness, a hazy blur of nothingness appeared, tempting him to sleep and so avoid the crisis. But no! How could he face expectant eyes tomorrow and talk only of sleep! Oh hell! hell!

Omoh then heard a voice out of the not too distant past, reminding him that oftentimes duplicity turned out to be the best of policies. Why not? What the hell! that was the answer. And so he decided (once again) to build his castle according to the blueprints of his more experienced friend and trusted guide.

First of all, to stretch out as if he were asleep and (while stretching) to turn around and (while turning so—in her direction, of course) to lift the right arm up as if to scratch the head and (after scratching so) to let the arm fall slowly (so as in sleep-time) upon the body next to him (quite unintentionally like that) and—

Chree—ist! Not there! not there—upon her breast. Jee—sus! I could feel the bloody nipple burning a hole in the palm of my hand. I've got to move it. Jeese! my heart! it's pounding too hard. I've got to move my hand.

But then, suppose she should wake up! she would certainly think that I deliberately put my hand there. Shit! Shit!

Anyhow, she hasn't moved a hair. Perhaps she's fast asleep. Then why should I worry? Why shouldn't I just enjoy it while I can.

Thinking such things (and despite the pleasure that he felt), Omoh could not completely shut out the voices that he heard—those voices from a much more distant past of Sunday school and catechisms, of confirmation and confession (not Roman Catholic, but High Church Anglican), of parental admonitions and whaling leather straps. The hot sweat of passion, mingled with the colder sweat of fear and guilt, flowed freely from his forehead and gathered into trickles that tickled irritatingly.

Then (once again) the soft chiming telling the passing of another quarter hour reached his ears. That time, however, it dispelled the ghostly but insistent voices and intensified the tension of the moment. A sudden rising of the bird of dawn between his legs proclaimed (though silently) the fullness of the blood tide. Alas! he could not still the painful throbbing of the erected thing. Besides, his hand shook more violently than before.

Good God! if it should burst and spill the searing juices of his long frustrated passion! Should she then awaken, how would he explain the odd ejaculation? If not, how would he later in the morning explain the dark revealing stain that would be left there. How could—

But questioning, completely overwhelmed by long suppressed desire, quickly subsided. His hand, completely on its own now, rubbed lightly on the swollen nipple, tracing out small agitated circles. And now and then a much excited finger would press upon it and push it back into the soft jello of flesh from which it had grown. Then (sure enough) the other fingers, jealous of success, would emulate their fellow and close in firmly on the entire breast.

Quite intoxicated, Omoh felt a lightness in his head, a tightness in his loins and a weakness where his knees usually resided. He did not even hear the chiming of the distant clock intrude upon the brittle stillness of the room. And even if he had, he would not have recognized a sound so alien to the suspended motion of his world—world without end (for so it seemed to him). But then—

My God! I'm sure I heard her sigh. What now? She's coming awake! And now—now she's moving! Slowly but surely. Jee—sus! She's coming closer—closer to me. Shit!

Okay now, hold strain—hold strain. Perhaps she sleeping still. Aha, perhaps she dead to the world, but just moving in she sleep. Oh Lord! she right up against it now! Keep still—keep still, you stupid prick! You goin' bore through she flesh—she sof' sof' flesh?

Aha! you see, she fas' asleep. Buh Jeese, it feel so good. Mm-m-m, so damn good, man. Ah wish she would really wake up and feel good too, and move wid me—instead o' lyin' dere like deadwood.

Buh she ain't dead, man, she ain't dead at all. 'n fact she hot like hell. And a could feel de heart-beat underneat' de jelly, man.

Hey! what de hell! she can't be sleeping. Oh no, the prick goin' soon break off. Oh boy, she movin' laka pro. Hey! watch it! easy now, easy. Buh wha' happenin' now? Now she really waking up. Oh lord, she pushing me 'way. Wha' really happenin'? Now she tunning round—an' pullin' me 'gainst she! Migod, buh she strong bo—she hol'ing me too close—a can't breathe properly! Migod oh, she goin' stifle me 'against she breas' dem. O lord, she rough bo. Eh eh! Wha' de hell a-

124

happen? she grabbing fuh me boy and pullin' me on top a-she! Jee—ee—sus Chree—ist!

Omoh could feel himself about to black out. Poor prick! He felt it wedged firmly between her thighs. And then—a moistness searing blearing screaming deep deep into the fires of infernal darkness and still further down—further—further—coming—coming for to carry—coming—

The siren-voice, unheard up to that point, began to coo and murmur pleasant but inarticulated sounds. The hands, no longer talonlike, touched lightly here and there, casting a magic spell. And then, the gentler rotating of less rigid hips and subtle undulating of unknotted stomach muscles proclaimed a happy voyage.

Omoh could feel the definite acceleration of the roller coaster that speeds up up and onwards—upwards onwards—upwards onwards—coming coming (this time without sleep)—coming faster faster—coming for to carry—coming—com—

Shit! Shit! Shit! No! No! Not now! Not now! Take me! Oh take me please—plu-ea-ea-ease!

(bow wow) go away (bow wow bow wow) go away you silly monster (bow wow bow wow) please take me with you dear (down you silly bastard) shit (can't you recognise me yet) shit shit (knock knock) what the hell (Curly! knock knock) why me (wake up you fucking whore) why was i pushed away (knock knock knock Curly!) just at the very moment (keep still Omoh it's okay) what (just the milkman) who (Curly! wake up you bitch) what's happening (ok ok i'm coming i'm coming) who's coming (i'm coming) not me (thought i told you not to come here) come (without calling first) whose whispering (Curly you witch) which witch (open the fucking door) a witch (you're drunk) me drunk (go away or i'll call the cops) cops (really) jesus (yes) what did i get myself into (cops! for your husband) husband (that was long ago) good god (but you still call me when the heat's on) i got to get out (go away you son of a bitch) my Curly of the siren-voice (got some stud in there) okay that's it (or are you getting it from that mastiff over there) good god she's telephoning (okay i'm going) she's stopped thank god (goodbye dear Curly) sounds as if he's crying (you always were a bitch) good god he's really crying (but i'll always love you) poor man (bye anyhow) he's gone (bastard) now he has shut the gate behind him (shit of a man) my Curly (next time i'll kill him) she's coming back (shit) she's coming back.

"What's the matter, Curly?" Omoh softly inquired. "What was all that about?" hoping that there was some small chance that the magic of the recent past might be recaptured.

"Nothing, just some drunk good-for-nothing bum!"

"Gee, I was worried. I actually began to put my clothes on," he explained. Hearing nothing in response, he added, "I thought of coming to your aid in case he should get rough, but—but then I heard him claim to be your husband."

Hearing nothing still, he then inquired, "Is he really, Curly?"

"Is who what?" the question exploded.

Startled by the unaccustomed hardness of the voice—the recent siren-voice, Omoh remained silent for a while. Asking, "Are you feeling okay, dear?" he slowly approached, intending to console her.

But an unexpected retort stayed his anxious feet, "Why don't you finish dressing, Omoh, and get out of my house."

Frozen in his half dress, Omoh eventually inquired, "You really mean that, Curly?" in a subdued voice.

"Yes! Yes, I mean it, boy. Why don't you just fuck off and leave me alone."

Dazed and unbelieving, Omoh turned about and shuffled like an aged bear to the chair on which his clothes lay strewn. Automatically, like a tin man creaking at the joints, he slowly dressed himself. Then, sighing like a lion of faint heart, he stumbled upon straw legs out of the enchanted room.

As he departed he did not even hear the sobbing of the one-time fairy princess who, lured into the ordinary world of everyday occurrences, had turned into a witch. Even if he had he would not have understood the meaning of her tears, for he himself was still the ugly frog who had come close to being made a prince.

Out into the early morning chill walked Omoh, no longer caring to avoid the monstrous guardian of the gate. Nothing mattered then. Not even whether he was walking still, nor whither he was going. Everything seemed lost—completely lost.

* * *

Now I have told you all I know and all that I am sure Omoh would have wanted me to tell you. I know that he himself would have gladly told you all (just as he once told me himself) had he been able to.

Instead, he sits there at his desk humped forward like a toad, staring at the nothingness he saw and felt that very night. In fact, his face bedewed with perspiration reflects the wetness of the light rain that began to fall as he emerged out of the decaying garden plot.

But see! he stirs and reaches for an empty sheet of paper. His eyes, red with the intensity of feeling, project themselves far out as if to scan the unfamiliar regions he has so far avoided. Upon the much tormented face, a strange demonic glow appears. His fingers, trembling violently,

126

can hardly control the mechanism of the typewriter before him. And a murmuring from deep within his throat comes rumbling to the surface.

I think that it is time for me to go. Indeed, I must be off. I've overstayed my time. And so, farewell my friends. I would have liked to lift him up and take him into bed that he might rest more comfortably. But now I daren't. And so, once more, farewell. Adieu.

* * *

PART FOUR
A Non-ending

All the shapes you can ever see in your mind's eye. . . .
I was one of them. . . . I was dreaming.
No, God knows, I was never so wide awake.

Wilson Harris

Walking (drip) walking (drip drip) walking on (drip drip drip) and on and on (drip drip drip drip) not even feeling the wetness of the lightly dripping rain (sigh!) nor seeing the blackness of the early morning (yea though i walk) nor hearing the awful silence (in the shadow) and not caring (of the valley) about anything (of death) but knowing somehow

on such days and in such places one could go walking on and on (not thinking and not wondering) not stopping but just walking (but knowing somehow) on and on and on

walking drip walking drip drip on and on drip drip drip then seeing bright lights coming fast in all their glory to drive away the whee drip shadows from the valley and fearing no drip drip evil now but hearing not at my back but just ahead the drunken squeal of tires upon the drip drip asphalt coming fast within a blazing onrush of brightly shining chrome that does not heed protective hands but pushes by to bump and hurl the whee frail body soaring lightly upwards into the drip cool morning air that greets the startled eyes with dancing dark red twinkle twinkle stars that hail the little jimcrow who holds himself though wingless upside down for long fractions of a second before the sudden rockdrop down on to the pavement with back-cracking impact and

What is your name? (just walking on) Who the hell are you? (without thinking) Hey man! what is your name? (my name is n. or m.) Wonder who he is. (the inheritor of the kingdom of heaven) Cut the shit out, man! (a child of grace) Answer me, you bastard! (art thou he that took me from my mother's womb) Son of a bitch! (I have become a monster unto many) He's not dead, his eyes are open. (but my trust is in thee) At least he could show some signs of recognizing us. (outward and visible) Here's pen and paper, write your name down. (of an inward and spiritual grace) Say something, nigger! (—

130

Look, we're wasting time. A crowd is gathering and it's nearly morning. Let's write him up any old way—nobody'll care a damn.

Name: too many aliases to record.

Place of abode: a vagrant, of no fixed abode, belonging nowhere.

Occupation: drifting, with no visible means of support.

Time and Place: too early in the morning and too deep in the suburbs for the likes of him.

Destination: up to no good—perhaps on the way to commit—

(alas thou writest bitter things against me and makest me to posses my former iniquities for my soul is full of trouble i feel again the sinful lust of flesh i suffer more acutely of the foul decay not of the fraud and malice of the devil but of my own carnal will and frailness)

Is he badly hurt or is he dead? (in the midst of life we are in death) What can we do to help him? (for since by man came death) Call an ambulance! Quick! (by man came also the resurrection) What a damned shame! Imagine such a young—

whee whee the music sounds within my ear whee whee coming fast and once again the sound of squealing tires and too bright lights unveiling ghostly shadows of the dark and coming fast with revolving halo or red flashing light coming coming whee whee for to carry—coming for—coming

Okay now, make way there! Move over now. My God, his skull's cracked open! (break not the bruised reed) Be careful there, he's bleeding like a stuck pig. (nor quench the smoking flax) We've got to hurry. (but make him to hear of joy and gladness) Christ! he's all twisted up. (that the bones which thou hast broken may rejoice) Hey! wait a minute! what is his name? (name my name is) What the hell are you guys trying to do? You all call yourselves protectors of the people? The

131

guy's dying! (be thou my stronghold) Watch it, fella, we've got a job to do, you know. (whereunto i may always resort) My report first and anything afterwards, friend.(thou has promised me to help me) Shit on you and your goddam job, we've a life to save. (for thou are my house of defence) Easy now, easy. Now shut the door and hit it!

What a damned shame! Wonder where his mother is. (man is born of woman but hath a short time to live) Jesus! and so young. (he cometh up and is cut down like a flower) Hurry man, hurry! (he fleeth as it were a shadow) Hurry, if you want to save his life. (and never continueth in one stay) Jesus! How horrible!

* * *

whee whee along the merry go round of avenues and streets whee whee whee whee down through the labyrynth of city streets whee whee screech screech that keeps the monster hidden whee whee limp body strapped down tight against the whee whee lurchings and the whee whee hustling of the roller coaster coming faster and whee-ee-ee faster swing low sweet chariot whee whee screech screech coming for to carry limp body throbbing here and throbbing there and throbbing everywhere with pain whee whee sweet pain that promises deep sleep swing low sweet sleep deep sleep like a drug sleep that doesn't stupefy whee whee a band of angels coming whee whee for to carry limp body that hardly feels the pulsebeat nor the heartbeat deep within whee whee coming after broken body strapped tight within the scree-ee-eeching flash flash chariot throbbing with the heavy pulsebeat of engine idling as the silent whirling of the flash flash red light loudly proclaims the moment's urgency flash flash and now (easy there) being gently borne aloft and (steady now steady) hurried down long corridors clip clop clip clop (who's he what happened) on through the softly swinging doors until

now a band of angels coming coming dressed in white and faceless but staring without smiling through narrow slits of eyes and coming coming for to carry

now being carried on through other swinging doors one and then another on and on into a searing blearing whitelight of room much brighter than the tropic glare of sunlight and

voices now voices not loud nor whispering but soft and firm amidst the tinkle tinkle silver stars and swishy swishy laundered uniforms and voices voices coming closer coming louder into my tinkle tinkle swish swish world and coming for to

and now out from the faceless blur twin slits of eyes appear steel-cold and blue just like those silver pieces neatly lain out in full array upon a nearby table dressed in white just like the watchful band of angels round about and coming closer closer for

and higher up much further up a closer circle of much larger eyes huge steel-rimmed eyes look down not blinking winking and not nodding kindly but fixed with an empty gaze defying anyone to pry into the mystery of the argus lights that pierce the scene below

and voices voices once again now speaking words about the broken body that hardly feels the pulsebeat heartbeat deeper down but hears the voices observe how strange it is that one so full of rhythm once like all the others of his ilk should be so deathly still now (there's a brown boy in the ring tra la la la la la) and wondering (come show me yuh motion tra la la la la) if perchance (can't show yuh me motion tra la la la la la) he would pull through (but sure would if i could ha ha ha ha) and

133

and now being whirled and twirled upon a swirling tide of air and seeing dimly in the bright light everything and everyone slowly dissolve into a fascinating blur of formlessness and then begin to fade far far away and then

   and then sweet nothingness and peace deep peace and nothingness not even pain nor sleep sleep that doesn't stupefy but

   but just sweet nothingness sweet nothing nessnor

* * *

now i lay me down oceandeep in whalegut of space black shipwomb tomb of distinguishable shapes forgotten wraiths persistent rot of time everlasting heartbeat pulsebeat all acrumble collapsing rumbletumble into total blackout fadein fadeout mergein mergeout spinning spinout emerging in kaleidoscope of forms that

   what is your name your name who are you you who are you your name you must be able to say what your name is who are you you must be able to be able

   able able able rings a bell a bell a bell rings abel abel abel empty shell of skull battered shattered skull awkward grinning skull with broken body lying limp and rigoring alongside branch-burning firepile much brighter than thin spiralling of smoke from smouldering bushheap where nearby stands another twin brother of the other but unfallen masking with flytrap of smile the demonself within

   cain cain standing uptall and smiling sweet like other cane cane plump with syrup of black islandsoil cain cane twinbrother of the other risen stirruphigh astride a spotted gelding greyred legstained with bloodbrain beside blackburning canebush masking with flytrap of

134

smile the demonself that hears the vain complaint of flies fastfleeing the blackbuzzing fountainhead of skull cleansplit by flashing hooves but gloats upon the secret glory of the sooty stalks

cain cane sugar of name cane cain dissolves resolves dissolves resolves again fadein fadeout mergein mergeout in what your name is who you are again another frame spinning spinout

dahomey roomy kingdom where came cane twinbrother of cane and the other cain standing uptall amidst the tiny blacksunburnt offshoots of the massive fatherhulk recent kingfigure hunter-fisher lain low by distant bulletblow to trusting woolhead foolhead dead beside still smouldering cookfires

blackcracked woolskull awkward hanging foolskull fadein fadeout mergein mergeout emerge in spinning spinout of forms imposed one on the other in multiframe of namegame who you are what your name is

goman pawman dingman koroman tynman papaman boman egoman rotyman dingoman aribman arackman wrackman cribman awman fadein fadeout mergein mergeout fleshin fleshout emerge in name of manykind man mandingo and papawman carib and arawackman eboe and keromantyn a ring a bell and cane game

now i lay me down whaledeep in oceangut of space black shipwomb constricting tomb of forgotten wraiths indistinguishable shapes fishpacked shelfstacked clampcramped crackbacked paindrained with flux itchrich with pox flowercovered with thickshit and retching stenchdrunk with persistent rot of heartbeat pulsebeat amidst longborning deaths fastdying births

blackcramped woolskull packedtight retching crackedskull fadein fadeout mergein mergeout in spinning spinout of images imposed one on the other in multicoloured frame of who your name is what you are

redspattered deadskull longhaired sandfilled splitskull twisted from bronze tightsinewed body lowlylying beside smouldering shorefires where nearby standing uptall a helmetfitted figure another cain twinbrother of the other canecains masking with flytrap of smile and piety the demonself that hears the vain complaint of squawwife bewailing recent mankill

now i lay me down oceandeep in whalegut of space black shipwomb of forgotten wraiths familiar shapes persistent rot of time everlasting heartbeat pulsebeat spinning spinout mergein mergeout fleshin fleshout emerge in vivid images of what your name is who you are

gianttall sons of earthmen sweatglistening pantherman of ancient royalty slowmoving up steeprising freezewhitetopped mountainhome from where slowoozing springs thintrickling seek oneanother then meeting soon shootoff fastrunning rumbletumble asplintering against the raggedjagged rockface then reuniting plunging plumbdown sheerdrop into the frothfringed pool beneath then soon reappearing far less hurryscurry along the grassy flatland on to the distant oceanhome and subsequent rebirth in purer form

and there poised readysteady on the bankland smaller spearbearing earthmen at huntandfishing lifegame mudsmeared jungledarlings fierceflashing eyes agleaming with the knowledge of all things acient wisdom out of ancient mudhead

black freezewhitetopped mountain slowclimbing sweating tallmen small headandfacesmeared mudmen splinterhealing headstream fastfeeding fishstream flowing flowout spinning spinout emerge in hot windswirling sandland in flatland teeming with lightfooted fat herds in

sweltering treetangled rainland a onceuponatime old birthland ancient
rootland a still unbroken chainland of scattered strandlands sunlands
recalling ancient mudland

and now i lay me down muddeep in whalegut of space black ship-
tomb womb of forgotten wraiths familiar shapes persistent rot of time
everlasting pulsebeat heartbeat of time spinning spinout emerge in
ancient centerearth child ancient nightandday child ancient lifeand
death child not mythic edenfield child but springyoung and winteraged
child summerfull and autumnripe child lifeoutofdeath child a whatyour-
name is child a manynamegame child omchile mochile mohchile
homchile omoh/homo a manandwoman manchile a cainandabelkind
chile a manykindofman chile

* * *

now let me tell you who i am rather let me introduce myself my name
is omoh/homo child of island man and woman induced by childhood
dreams to come here to the big land and i had thought of telling you all
that happened since the day of my arrival and to explain why now i sit
here in this tiny room shut in from the light of day in an alien land

but now there is no longer need to tell you anything in fact i have no
time to spare i must bestir myself arise and leave my prison i must get
up and if i fall get up again fall down get up again and so to hold the head
up high

and now indeed i try to rise slowly now slowly i feel the pain and
indeed the pain grows worse a gutdeep pain a wombdeep kind of pain
black pounding pain impending blackout headpain and now indeed i
feel my eyes grow dark and i begin to fall down for fall i must yet despite

137

the pain i must pull up myself so so ah a little more there there not so bad now but still it hurts and i must still endure the painful issuing forth of being out of shattered self and so defeat the cold umcompromising grasp that strives to hold me down fallen out of life down into the very core of life i must arise now life out of death and be myself anew aha there there up up so so a little more and right up now and then a step forget the silly eyedrops that irritate the cheeks another step now despite the unaccustomed legs another there and another and so to walk again slowly but surely to keep on walking that is at least until the certain stoptime and then perhaps to walk in other lands and in other forms i know not of so far

* * *

Should you

shatter the door
and walk
in the morning
fully aware

of the future
to come?
There is no
turning back

Edward Brathwaite

PART FIVE
An Unexpected Commentary

Each of us now held at last in his
arms what he had been for ever
seeking and what he had eternally
possessed.

Wilson Harris

Ah yes, Omoh got up, walked out of his room and so escaped the undertow of past experiences that almost overwhelmed him. He sits there now reclined within the mural-decorated cabin, hearing without paying much attention to the pleasant droning of the whisper jet, hurtled along by the backward thrusting of engines poised precariously beneath lightly vibrating wings.

Ah yes, he sits there now feeling the impending curtain-fall of heavy eyelids, but remembering and feeling all within his still aching limbs and hearing, in the distance, a band of angels fast approaching, coming for to carry the sometimes up sometimes down self on to peaceful sleep—deep sleep, like a drug that doesn't stupefy.

Ah yes, he sits there now reclined with legs folded at an awkward angle within the narrow seat-space. But I no longer feel the urge to pick him up and take him to bed that he may sleep more comfortably. For I, despite my full knowledge of his past and strong compassion for him, could never have affected the necessary unravelling of his knot of self. Instead, I watch him sitting there, remembering all and seeing all besides:

the rigid brown face once pleasant but now staring up defiantly at the ceiling and ignoring completely the timidly approaching boy all dressed up in black and puzzled by the alien hush within the house filled with family and visitors—

the round smiling face bent forward in the act of writing and revealing an intriguing bald spot to the adolescent youth more fascinated now by the thin sweeping upstrokes and thicker downstrokes that form the legal words upon the pages there before it—

the black leather-face burnt dry by hot sea-spraying winds and the rope-bitten hands waving a temporary farewell to the wrinkled face wizened with fourteenth round of childbirth but still undaunted there on the shore with the little boy who worships the old man who sails out far beyond the ken of ordinary eyes only to disappear and never to return that day or any other—

the high cheekbones of narrow face gazing with pride upon the schoolboy there before the steaming fishbroth and wondering why instead of eating he sits there musing in the presence of fuller sister face and brother face even more bronze and bursting with the zest for life and ready to entertain at any time with local bobby burns verse created on the spot but never married just like the sisters with whom he shares a full but simple life—

the tiny yellow crinkled seed of face with blood-red eyes squinting from the smoke of ever-puffing corn-cob pipe and protecting the mystery of the frail body covered thick with layers of underclothes despite the heat and smiling at the tiny frog-eyed boy who like the others of the family wonders where she comes from each sun-rising morning and goes each sun-setting time—

the more vivid mother face resolving furrowed wrinkles of concern into spontaneous laughter or sparkle-eyed with satisfaction as fast-clicking needles release the final stitches of some piece of finery and father face more stern in attitude of discipline and no-nonsenseness yet on occasion betraying a subtle smiling and mischievous recalling of much cherished secrets—

Ah yes, Omoh sits there, remembering all and seeing all and feeling all swing low sweet chariot, not hearing the light snoring that issues from his lips but smiling peacefully and remembering the band of angels, forgotten faces of his island-past, coming for to carry him to rockland pounded each day by mountain waves of ocean round about and burnt coconut-branch brown by the shimmering rays of sun and echoing loudly with the buzzing sounds of stinging insects, sleep-waking disharmonies of cock-crowing and dog-barking.

Ah yes, Omoh sits there hearing a band of angels coming for to carry his sometimes up sometimes down self home to the little rock that each night disappears quite swallowed up after the briefest twilight into the womb of night but reappears each day at earliest sunlife to let the motley crowd perform again, with new intensity, their carnival of life.

Ah yes, swing low sweet chariot, a band of angels coming—coming for to carry Omoh home to kiss Ma Poppo, Janice and Mildred.

141

AFTER FORWARD
by Hugh Hood

CLOSE HARMONY: LORRIS ELLIOTT'S
NARRATIVE COUNTERPOINT

In the novel *Coming for to Carry* Lorris Elliott has produced a tour de force of narrative strategy which clearly reflects his own musical interests and powers. The book is an exercise in the establishment of inner voices, continuing musical sequences of tones which sound together, as in classical counterpoint, giving the listener (it is important that much of the novel be read aloud with great care) or the silent reader an impression of different voices speaking simultaneously in such a way as to be intelligible in themselves, and more intelligible and meaningful when heard in concert with other voices.

The book tells a simple, familiar story, as the surface voice or "lead" of the narrative. A young man called Omoh who may be a native of one of the smaller Caribbean islands of the size of, say, Tobago, leaves the somewhat larger island which has been his home for several years to fly to "the big land", a country never precisely identified, much like Canada. On the day of departure from "the Rock" he is accompanied to the airport by many friends and lovers, especially old Ma Poppo, and a pair of girl friends, Janice and Mildred, who love him dearly. Departure time approaches; the flight is announced; and in his haste to board the aircraft Omoh neglects to kiss the girls goodbye. This significant lapse in good manners and charity becomes a sign of a primordial wrongdoing for Omoh, a fall which his conscience cannot admit or control. The action of the narrative then becomes the wide circle of departure and return, bringing Omoh (homo, man in general) back in the angelic chariot of death to the girls and the sweet innocence of youth. There is something of Tennessee Williams in the conception.

So far the story seems banal, predictable, not worth close attention, but the sense of having failed at one's first task of faithfulness and generosity, in the conscience of the central character, is exhibited with tact and precision. At first the story simply takes Omoh to a university in a city on the extreme west coast of North America, possibly Vancouver. Some geographical indications that we are in Vancouver are supplied but the point is not insisted on; the geography of the novel doesn't serve a naive realism. We follow Omoh through two university years, his gradual acclimatisation, his discovery of winter — which, surprisingly, he doesn't seem to mind too much; a cliché of this familiar story is wisely avoided. Omoh shares a basement apartment with his fellow islander Kopakie. He rides around the city in the big blue torpedo-shaped Nash automobile of another friend, Big Jay.

The Nash possesses that interesting feature which used to be advertised as "Bed-in-a-car." Its seats fold back and down to form a neat double bed, for campers or other recliners. This feature of the Nash was part of American automotive folklore for many years; it is introduced very fittingly. The car may at any moment be transformed into a bed but never is. The young men in the blue torpedo never find any occasion to transform their chariot into a sleeping chamber or a place for love. They lead lonely, alienated, anonymous lives, and the strain tells.

The work begins to deploy its narrative ingenuity at the point where Omoh has acquired a home, if only a temporary one, some sort of identity as a university student, and a few friends, including an elderly lady upstairs who is surprisingly forbearing, friendly and decent to the young man. This temporary identity serves as the surface of the music for the remainder of the action, but its coherence is questioned, and crossed, by voices below the surface. The narrative line begins to resemble coaxial cable, the thick powerlines used by the telephone company to transmit many messages at once. We remember suddenly and shockingly that the central part of the story was preceded by poetic statements in other voices, that a first-person narrator has intruded on the action from time to time, that Omoh's story is being watched from a point outside its action and beyond it, that this outside voice knows what the end of the story has been and will be. In the first person narrator's voice we hear echoes of island history, of the torment of exile, the necessity of dying to return. The book grows ominous.

At a point past the middle of the action Omoh becomes seriously involved with pixy-like golden Curly, a woman of ripe sexual attraction, something of a forbidden goddess. We infer that she is a white woman, but with real tact the narration refrains from insisting on colour difference, which is treated as irrelevant; the book is not a work of sociology. Omoh courts Curly in the course of a series of misadventures which might be comic if the musical structure were not so dense and bewildering. Confused voices surface in Omoh's consciousness. He goes for long moments without knowing what voice is speaking through his mind. He lapses into sequences of impressions in which he becomes curiously depersonalised. At length he arrives in Curly's apartment as an accepted suitor, where his goddess serves him a meal of steak.

Omoh has no developed taste for this North American delicacy. He doesn't know how the thick slices of meat are prepared for the table, and when asked how he wants his steak cooked — given the usual three choices — he replies, "Rare," thinking that Curly is a rare woman; her food must be rare too. His meal is served to him and the nicely browned surface of the meat deceives him. He slices into it deeply, and the blood and juice flow out, repelling and sickening him; these foreign delicacies are not to his taste. The scene is delivered with real power.

At this point the "lead" narrative voice, the top line of the music, as it were, becomes submerged in more turbulent voices from the depths of man's self. Omoh arrives in Curly's bed to fall into chaotic dreams from which he is awakened by her harsh dismissal. He cannot understand her explosive cruelty. He is left alone. Other sounds in his consciousness obliterate his identity. In a striking prose poem which concludes the book, Omoh is brought back in a dream-flight to his point of departure and the circuit of travel is perfected. The chariot has carried him back to Janice, Mildred, and old Ma Poppo.

The narrative attains its peculiar excellence in the constant interruption of the melody by the inner voices. Sometimes we are vividly reminded of the methods of Joyce, and from time to time a voice like that of the American poet Hart Crane is established in the music. Perhaps Hart Crane's personal story is appropriate to the story of Omoh, for Crane died a suicide in the Caribbean.